The People of the Bird

A Novel

Written and Illustrated by

Mike Jelliffe

NENGE SERIES – Book One

NENGE BOOKS
Australia

The People of the Bird
by Mike Jelliffe

Published by NENGE BOOKS, Australia.
ABN 26809396184
Email: nengebooks1@gmail.com

Cover and illustrations by Michael A Jelliffe

Nenge Books welcomes authors interested in publishing. We publish quality books for independent authors using print n demand technology.

Paperback ISBN-13: 978-0-9925620-0-7

Also available as an e-book.

e-book ISBN-13: 978-0-9925620-1-4

*Dedicated to the people of PNG
who have lost their land and heritage
in the wake of resource exploitation.*

Table of Contents

Sketch of Moi River area — not to scale

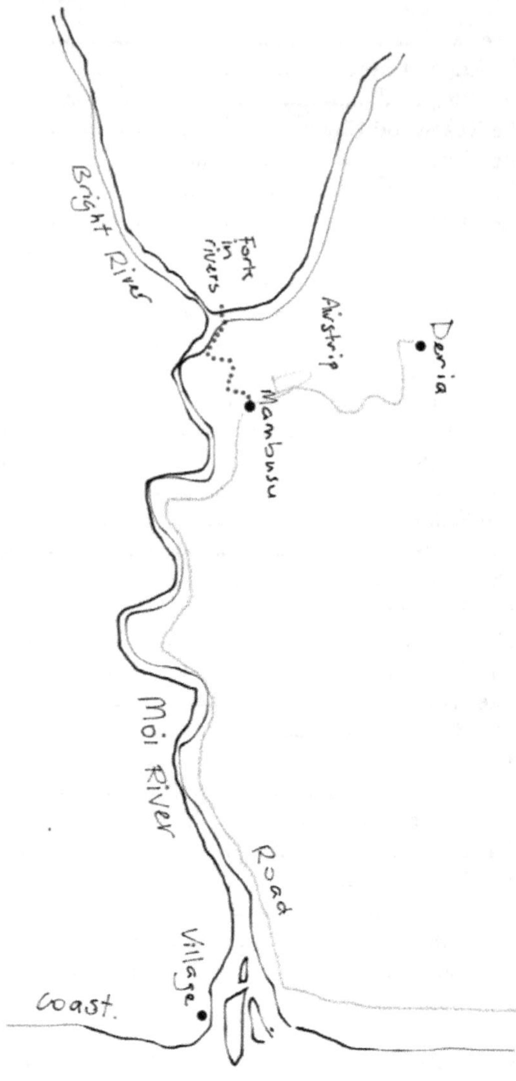

Bright River
Fork in rivers
Airstrip
Denia
Mambusu
Moi River
Road
Village
Coast.

Preface

Melanesian culture is reflective. At its core are assumptions about the past – the 'tumbuna lain' of ancestors. These stories of the past are traditionally enshrined in sacred and secret narratives, revealed only to the initiate. There is a sense that each clan has a destiny to pass on this narrative to the next generation. By doing so it preserves its integrity and the clan's identity.

But this culture is also progressive. It recognises that the land is not just for this generation; it's for those to come. Children are treasured and parents devote themselves to doing all they can to ensure their children receive the best education and opportunity for their future. They control the destiny of their children. Their heritage is also their children's heritage.

Unfortunately, in modern PNG the things that used to be considered as a heritage for the next generation - land and the culture and lifestyle associated with it - are being stolen from the next generation by the mercenary march of exploration, mining and logging as well as modernity. Greed and profit (where there's a difference) have fueled the fallacy that cash payments today are richer than the land and its heritage tomorrow.

There's a temptation to try and remain in the past, and let the ancient stories hold us back in that past. But we can't live in the past today; we can only learn from it and live by looking to the future. So how much better is it when the ancient wisdom can be harnessed to inform contemporary issues, projecting us into a future that is rooted in this wisdom of the elders, yet forging a pathway for success in the modern world.

This novel is the story of how the legacies of two ancestors, enshrined in a written narrative and in oral traditions, inform and guide present generational leaders as they face the challenges of massive change through the coming of a mining venture to their community. I hope it raises some of the questions that local communities may need to ask more aggressively when faced with a similar challenge.

I wish to thank my ever-patient wife for her ability to put up with my dreams and ideas, including writing this story. Any success of this novel is attributed to her. I also thank the members of my family and good friends in Australia and PNG who gave me the kind of honest feedback that helped refine the text. I particularly thank Ray Budge and Phil Fitzpatrick for their reviews and feedback. My thanks also to the many people across Papua New Guinea who have become friends and *wantoks* over the four decades that I have been privileged to be associated with them. They have taught me so much about culture and life. This story is but a reflection of some of the things I have learned from them.

Mike Jelliffe
Mt Hagen, April 2014

Chapter 1

The Rugby Game

My love affair with Papua New Guinea (PNG) really started with a game of rugby.

1972. I was sixteen. The memory is as sweet as life was then. A rabble of pimply-faced schoolmates had gathered in front of the school sports notice board, scrutinising a type-written list recently pinned on it. Elbowing my way past them I searched for my own name, and found it. *Justin L. Orlando – Wing.* I'd been selected in the inter-school team to visit New Guinea. I was ecstatic and yelled and jumped and punched the air with joy!

My Australian private boys school joined other schools each year in a state consortium to send a Rugby team to play in the Territory of Papua and New Guinea. Becoming a member of this elite team was the holy grail of high school rugby, and it was now in my hands!

Sport, particularly rugby, was the main source of masculine activity and peer advancement at private schools such as mine, and I excelled. Blessed with a good build, I was proud of my physical prowess, demonstrated most comfortably and successfully on the football field. I tanned easily, kept it during winter, and must admit to some pride in meeting most expectations of the stereotype Aussie pin-up boy of the era – bronzed, athletic and well muscled.

Except for my Italian heritage, though I kept that hidden as much as I could even though it was several generations distant. Private schools were for good Anglo-Aussie families. The migrant kids went to state schools. So I never disclosed my middle name, *Lupiano,* in case it betrayed me. It was tradition now in our family that every firstborn son carried this family name, a tradition initiated apparently by my grandfather. So I grew up learning to practice racism but shielding myself from receiving it, though somehow this never seemed to sit comfortably with me.

The week of the tour was to be a turning point in my life, just three weeks after I turned seventeen. Looking back now, I would never have dreamed how it would change my life forever.

We boarded a rather tired looking TAA Boeing 727 at Brisbane Airport for the three-hour flight to Port Moresby. The immigration process was minimal because 'The Territory', as residents colloquially referred to it, was under Australian administration. When the aircraft door was opened at Port Moresby airport a tsunami of tropical heat swamped us, but we disembarked enthusiastically and walked across the tarmac to Jackson's Airport International Terminal, the heat like a hair dryer blowing in our faces. Welcome to the Territory!

We played four games that week and sweated a lot in the tropical climate. In our free time, excursions were made to visit some important cultural locations and events. Two of these stood out as significant for me.

The good people from Hanuabada village, the enigmatic village built on stilts over the waters of Port Moresby Harbour, staged a canoe race in their outrigger *lakatois,* with traditional dancing on shore. I remember being stunned by the graceful beauty of the bare breasted dancing girls adorned with shells and feathered head-dresses, long grass skirts swaying rhythmically to the beat of their hand held *kundu* drums, brown skin glistening in the tropical sun. And I vividly recall being captivated by this new culture, its colour and its people.

A visit to the Australian War Cemetery at Bomana just out of Port Moresby was a pensive opportunity to consider the cost of war, and the cost of freedom. Row after row of white crosses between immaculate lawns, enshrined in the history of a World War that I had so far paid little attention to.

My reflections did lead me to a greater appreciation of the Vietnam War that Australia had just disengaged from. At school, visits from returned Vietnam Vets had regaled us with horror stories of military operations against the Viet Cong. How could so many people die, on both sides, to try and maintain the ideal they fought so hard to keep? Would I ever be asked to stand up for an ideal with my life, I wondered?

Three rugby games were held in Port Moresby at various ovals in the city and were inconsequential. We won easily. The games attracted crowds of onlookers and it was obvious that rugby was a noble sport in the eyes of the local people. Our opponents outmatched us in physique but we had the upper hand in training and skills. Our manipulation of the ruck and ability to outpace our opponents in getting the ball along the back line to the wingers gave us most tries. Of course, being a winger, I bagged my share!

One game was different though, not the actual game so much as the location and circumstances. In an effort to promote a more regional perspective to our visit, the team was invited to play a representative rural team at a location several hours' drive out of Port Moresby. The game would require us to overnight at a village and return the next day.

It would be a great adventure.

Chapter 2

The Village

Our transport would be local Public Motor Vehicle (PMV) – a six-ton flat top Toyota truck with a tarpaulin covered seating rack on the back. It was able to carry about thirty people sitting on benches lengthways down the vehicle. In fact, we saw very few PMVs on the road with as few as thirty people on board. Most were overcrowded and had the centre section piled up with bags of produce, coconuts and root vegetables, sometimes livestock such as pigs, all bound for the markets in Port Moresby. Occasionally that produce overflowed onto the roof of the seating rack or behind the bull bar.

We were up at 5am waiting for the PMV. It was at least a half-day drive and we soon ran out of bitumen as we journeyed further along the coast and then started winding up into mountain country. The road became narrower and rougher, the bridges and river fords more precarious. But this was an adventure of a lifetime and our distaste for dust and gritty eyes were a small token price to pay. No one seriously complained.

The location had been chosen carefully to give us exposure to a more remote area away from the increasing urbanization of Port Moresby. The Moiaimba people of the area welcomed us like kings. *Leis* (necklaces) of frangipani flowers were placed around our necks and we seemed to shake everyone's hand at least once as the procession of local native people eagerly pressed around us.

A group of women and girls was dancing nearby. Though not nearly as elaborately dressed as their Hanuabaduan counterparts, they still exuberated such grace in their movement. Shuffling their feet in unison, small kundu drums beating out a monotone rhythm as they chanted, their grass skirts flipped left then right in time to the rhythm. I noted that even in the mountainous area we were now in, they wore necklaces of cowry shells and mother of pearl obviously not found locally. I'd learn later of the trading routes that crisscrossed the country, and the high value of seashells for highlands people.

The game was scheduled for early in the afternoon, just after we'd taken a short break from the road trip and eaten lunch. It seemed to me to be a great strategy for the other team! I don't think anyone in our team felt ready to play after so many hours sitting on wooden slats in the back of a PMV on winding dirt roads, and then a meal!

It didn't matter. The other team played courageously but seemed relatively untrained in the art of rugby. I scored three of our five tries when we switched the direction of the ball halfway out along the back line, and caught their defenses short on the blind side wing. We won effortlessly again, though did so in a fun spirit of friendship and camaraderie with our opposing team. They responded enthusiastically, playing as if their lives depended on it, and losing as if their new friendship with us demanded it.

There were few buildings made of permanent materials in the village, just the school building and a small trade store that looked like it'd been made from scraps left over from the school construction. The rest were of bush timber and *kunai* grass roof thatching. We were to lie out our sleeping bags on the floor of the two-room school. There were no washrooms - we washed in the river and used bush pit latrines especially constructed behind the village for our visit. Our evening meal was supplemented by local food – sweet potato, taro and some combinations of what they called sago wrapped in a banana leaf with pumpkin or banana. I didn't try everything on offer, but what I did, I enjoyed.

In the evening a large fire lit up the central area of the village and we sat round it while the villagers introduced us to some more of their culture. This time it was the men who danced. Elaborate costumes of feathers, shells, animal tusks and skins, and local vines that seemed to be held together with beeswax and bush twine. Yellow, red and orange ochres coloured their faces and bodies. The kundu drums continued their monotonous beat as some of the opposing rugby team members attempted to tell us the stories behind the dances.

"This is the dance we do before we go hunting *magani*, wallabies," my opposite winger, Abu, explained. "See, it looks like we're stalking the wallaby until we have surrounded it." Then suddenly the dancers leapt into the air, pretending to throw their spears at the wallaby.

Later, when another dance group began to entertain us, Abu interpreted again. "When we're hunting *kuskus*, tree possums," he whispered, "we smell the air for their distinct aroma." The dancers circled with their noses held high. "Then when we get their scent…. you'll smell it one day…. we find which tree it's in and cut down the tree with the kuskus in it. That way we can get the kuskus." The dancers mimicked the felling of a tree.

Then came a much more intense and less jovial dance. The dancers look quite threatening, their costumes and choreography much more serious and intimidating. Abu briefed me once more. "This one is for chasing evil spirits from the gardens," he said. "When our mothers go to the food gardens, we need to protect them from any evil spirits." This interaction of the earthly and the spiritual intrigued me; it seemed so natural to them.

Later, as we lay on our sleeping bags, the sound of rain as it moved down from the high mountains against the main ranges and consumed our valley soothed our weary bodies, and lulled us into dreamland. In my heart and mind I was in ecstasy as I thought back over the events of the day. But my body was in agony as it craved to shut down for the night. My body won.

The rain persisted all night. We woke to the sound of drizzle on the corrugated iron roof of the school, and zero visibility outside in thick fog. It created an aura of mystery that cocooned the village, the fog forming a shroud that could be seen but not felt.

Our plan to be back in Port Moresby by 3 pm for our last night in this amazing country was now looking uncertain. Word had arrived that swollen rivers had made some of the river crossings impassible, so we'd need to wait. I didn't mind. I'd already fallen in love with the place and would gladly stay here longer.

While the others in our team splashed around with the football outside, I was eager to find out more about life here for the Moiaimba people. A couple of the opposition team members, former high school students, and the local teacher, a middle-aged man named David Umbare, were the best at English and were keen to answer my questions. They seemed glad that someone was interested enough in them.

I gathered that few of the villagers spoke much English, but rather a rough bush English they referred to as Pidgin English, as well as a coastal trade language called Motu, and their own local language dialect. Some of the older men had apparently learned Pidgin during the war when they were active in helping allied troops in various places around the country. I recognised a few words, like "morning" for good morning, and some pronouns like "you" and "me". The rest seemed to be a massive corruption of English, often by just adding "-im" or "-pela" at the end of the word. They spoke it so fast I really couldn't understand anything in conversation though.

Their local language, Moiaimbamatu (I found it easier to break it up to pronounce, Moi-aim-ba-matu), was completely unique to the five or six thousand people in the area who had really only been introduced to the outside world in the 1920s.

"We had a few years of intrusion by some itinerant gold diggers," David Umbare told me, "seeking alluvial gold in the mountain streams, they said. We had no value for gold, so we didn't mind. Apart from occasional government patrol officers, the only others who'd shown any interest in us were missionaries. They made a walking visit into the area every two years, stayed for a few weeks to preach around the villages, and left again."

A couple of villages had built churches that suddenly filled with faithful parishioners again every two years.

"How long have your people lived here in this valley?" I asked.

"Well, it's hard to tell," replied David. "We don't measure time like you do, and we didn't keep records of births and deaths because no one counted the years. But our traditional stories seem to indicate that our forebears settled here about twelve generations ago." I did a quick count. Based on twenty-five-year generations, I estimated about three hundred years ago.

"Do you know where they came from?" I asked.

"You're a very inquisitive young man, Justin," David responded. "We appreciate you showing so much interest in us though. Our traditional stories, which is our history, tell us that they were coastal people who'd sailed from distant islands. That's why we're actually more like coastal people than highlanders in some of our customs. Perhaps they were running away from something, or perhaps they were looking for new land for farming, our stories tell us the answer to those questions."

I was surprised that while David knew the answer, he wasn't prepared to tell me. He saw the look on my face and continued.

"Our ancient stories are sacred to us. They're part of our identity, who we are, so unless you become part of our tribe, we can't disclose these stories to you."

I nodded to show that I understood. But really I didn't. We westerners share our history so freely. So I continued my questioning about more recent events.

Construction of the road in 1967 had been a landmark achievement that had finally allowed 4WD vehicle access to the area. With it came the importing of trade store goods, and a route to the coast and capital to sell produce. This also allowed a freedom of people movement that encouraged teachers to come to the area as well as saving high school students a three-day walk to the coast to attend boarding school.

There was still no high school in the area, and only one small primary school at the main village of Mambusu, where we stayed. David Umbare was one of the first Moiaimba to be able to complete Primary and limited High School education and be trained as a teacher, preferring to return to his home area rather than teach in the city.

Most intriguing though was the political dilemma faced by these people - what to do with Underpants! At first I was extremely puzzled by the term. Many of these villagers still wore more traditional clothing – grass skirts for the women and bark, shells and leaves tucked under a rattan belt for the men – I could bet they didn't even have a word for underpants in their vocabulary!!

With a little more coaxing I discovered from my new friends that 'Underpants' was a gross corruption, and misunderstanding, of the word Independence! The Australian Government had committed to fast tracking the handover of administration of the Territory to the people of Papua and New Guinea. Self-government was to be granted next year, 1973, and full Independence in 1975. It was clear that the Moiaimba people had little understanding of what was happening in the greater scenario of their country's emergence into the wider global community.

It was all over too quickly. The rivers had subsided enough by late morning and we set out for Port Moresby. As the village disappeared behind the first corner, once again hidden from the rest of the world, I felt a tinge of sadness, of loneliness, like I'd just left a good friend behind and didn't know how long before I'd see him again.

I realized that in actual fact I'd left part of my heart behind at Mambusu.

Chapter 3

The Rosewood Chair

When I arrived back in Australia after the rugby trip, nothing had been clearer to me than the desire to return to Papua New Guinea and make my life's work there. My newfound but short-lived friendships in Mambusu had awakened in me a desire to somehow assist these people. What I saw with my own eyes had stirred a consciousness that I could help make a difference, though how that could happen was a little vaguer.

After graduating from boarding school the following year, I enrolled in university, completing two degrees – in Political Science (majoring in Pacific Studies) and Environmental Studies (majoring in Community Development). These seemed to me to capture the two areas of greatest need I saw among the Moiaimba – to understand the political environment they were about to be engulfed in, and to know how to best be equipped to engage in the modern world with the natural resources they had at their disposal.

It also seemed that these degrees would be an appropriate way to gain employment in PNG, hopefully in an agency dealing with these kinds of issues. As it turned out, I was right. I was offered a job with the PNG Department of Social Resources within three months of completing my second degree.

Shortly before I booked my flight back to Port Moresby in 1978, my grandfather died. He was a kindly gentleman who'd lived on his own since his wife, my grandmother, had passed away nearly two decades earlier. I got the impression from somewhere that she was his second wife. I have only faint but happy memories of her. Grandfather was the one who'd insisted that I be named *Lupiano*. He had few possessions, preferring to live simply as his twilight years approached, though he did have one piece of furniture that I was to receive from his estate, with strict instructions that it was never to leave the family.

I'd never seen this chair at his house and learned that he'd kept it stored safely in his shed, in a plain timber and plywood container made specially to house it. The chair was, without overstatement, magnificent.

Constructed from rosewood, it had over the years acquired a deep maturity of rose red colour with a tinge of silver. The swirl of the grain was like etchings into the wood. Its design was most unusual. Ornate carvings decorated the armrests and front legs. A craftsman had spent hours meticulously creating this detail. The backrest was in-filled with rattan, and possibly the seat base originally also. This now had a cushion covered with an exotic tapestry like material, almost oriental in style. While the timber was just approaching its heyday, the material was unfortunately well past it.

I fell in love with the chair immediately and placed it in my bedroom for the few weeks before departing for PNG. There I could regularly enjoy its surprising comfort. It almost felt like it'd been made to fit my personal body shape. It would take pride of place in my house from now on.

Of course, common sense prevailed. It was impractical to take the chair to PNG, so I duly packed it away again and placed it in storage with my other remaining possessions. I would go to PNG without it.

Chapter 4

The Mine

Returning to PNG in 1978 was a dream come true. I'd followed the political growth of the country carefully and could name every government Minister and Departmental Secretary. I was intimate with both the political process and practical transition to self-government in 1973 followed by Independence in 1975.

I knew the name and vital statistics of every province. My environmental studies had also given me considerable background to the resources found in each, as well as the environmental problems being faced by the people in those provinces.

The Ok Tedi mine, situated in the far northern reaches of the Western Province in the shadow of the spectacular Hindenburg Wall and Star Mountains. Gold, copper and a huge tailings problem. Pollution from the project had already affected the Fly River that received, by way of tributaries, the effluent from the mine. By the late 1970s local people even at the mouth of the Fly River, hundreds of kilometres away, were reporting deformities in fish caught in the delta. Suspicion fell to cyanide poisoning – a key ingredient in the gold extraction process – which was to have a major polluting effect on the whole Fly River system.

Unrestrained logging in New Britain was leaving vast tracts of land stripped of all but a few trees. And of course, Bougainville's Panguna gold and copper mine, in the midst of political turmoil and tension as local Bougainvilleans reacted against the attitudes of the mine and the environmental pollution it also was causing. Who would have thought it would result in a civil war that would claim up to 20,000 lives, with the mine sabotaged and shut down by local revolutionary secessionist forces.

1998. The memories of that visit to Mambusu flooded back as I rounded the last corner into the village. Here I was back again, twenty-six years later. While I'd come on official business, I also had a personal agenda.

Papua New Guinea, as the country was christened on Independence Day, 16th September 1975, had won my heart. But I wanted to see if I could discover what it was about Mambusu and the Moiaimba people that had so crystallized within my spirit the desire to return.

In the last twenty years I'd worked my way up the ladder in the Department of Social Resources, from being a junior resource person to becoming a senior Manager. I'd been privileged to be involved in major projects such as Ok Tedi, Lihir and Misima gold mines, Freida River exploration and Ramu Nickel. Added to my knowledge of PNG was the experience of travel around the country to these places, and friends in all of them.

Achieving fluency in Pidgin English and Police Motu, still a major lingua franca of the coastal Papuan peoples, had been a major goal. Not content with "Aussie" Pidgin, I listened more than I talked, mimicked and practiced so that I spoke more like a local than a foreigner. I counted this as my most important asset in building relationships with the local communities I contacted. Needless to say, I rarely found anything other than total acceptance by community leaders wherever I went.

My primary role had always been in the area of liaison between the government and the local communities in the pathway of an exploration or mining project. In recent years that had included a role as Warden. Specifically it was to ensure that the government achieved its objectives while finding ways to keep the local people happy, and meet the legal obligations required under the Mining Act. We didn't phrase it like that of course. We used more 'govspeak', such as "ensuring equity for the local people and the government".

I say this somewhat sarcastically now because I've come to wonder if these two can actually be achieved together, or are they mutually exclusive? Can the government and shareholders gain what they want from the project, and the local people gain what they want at the same time? Despite my growing discontent with this philosophy of resource development, I maintained my commitment to try and gain the best outcome for the local people without compromising the government's key goals.

In fact I gained such a reputation for my ability to broker successful outcomes with local stakeholders that the Minister for Social Resources commended me. Of course, this only continued my upward spiral of promotion to hold a very senior position in the Department. New projects, with previously unimaginable scope, were beginning to be slated. The LNG project was about to move from years of exploration in the Southern Highlands and Upper Fly region of the Western Province to a massive project pumping liquid natural gas possibly to Australia.

New mines at places like Bundi in the Chimbu Province, and Frieda River in the Sepik, and several other new promising explorations, were starting to become visible on the country's resources radar. At the same time logging was actively eating away vast sections of virgin growth in a number of provinces. All these developments required active and successful liaison with the local communities involved. Most had been successful, a few not.

Our Department received advice of a project that was now preparing to develop after lying dormant in an exploration phase for some years. Following surveys of alluvial gold found in rivers in the area, the project principals proposed to develop a mine at the source of the gold deposits. The consortium would mine out the gold deposit, shown to also contain silver, in a manner similar to that used by Ok Tedi Mining. There Mt Fubilan was being reduced to rubble as it was chipped away to extract its mineral deposits of gold then copper, flushing the residue down the Fly River. The consortium alluded to using more environmentally friendly techniques for mining, though definition of these was hard to find in the company's initial proposal briefs.

I flicked through the proposal half-heartedly. I could see the battles looming as another mining Goliath, hand in hand with the Government, sought to find a way to patronize the local population, the David, without compromising on its shareholders' demands.

But suddenly this proposal had my full attention. The moment I turned the page to reveal the location, I recognised that this proposal was for the Namel Province. Specifically, it was on the land occupied by the Moiaimba people.

I began to read it much more carefully. Something tugged in my heart. I could visualize the issues these people would face in the next twenty years. Because most mines are still operating, the long-term impact on PNG communities cannot be studied historically beyond a relatively short time span.

There suddenly seemed to be so much at stake for the Moiaimba. This was a project I needed to be involved in.

I proposed to my Department Head that I be involved personally in the Namel mining proposal, and thankfully received his enthusiastic endorsement.

"In fact Justin," Kila had said, "I thought you'd be by far the best person in the Department to head this one up. I wanted to appoint you as Warden. You've proved yourself in that role, and seem to have perfected the ability to meet the local people with their expectations while keeping a firm grip on the government's plan. Let me know how I can help when you're ready."

"Wow," I mused, "for some reason this one seems to be a real challenge".

"Yeah," he continued, "This mine has the potential to be bigger than Ok Tedi or Lihir, but the logistical challenges in that rugged country are far greater than both those mines, except the place is a bit closer to Port Moresby. So it needs to be handled very sensitively or the local Moiaimba people will get upset and we don't want to risk another Bougainville or even minor sabotage."

So, I could now officially devote my entire attention to the Namel mine and the welfare of the Moiaimba people. For a few days I considered my options and then advised Kila that I had just two requests. He approved both.

I was ready for a holiday. My first request was for a month's leave, and so I booked a flight back to Australia.

Chapter 5

The Secret Diary

At forty-two years of age and unmarried, I enjoyed setting my own schedule when I could. It's not that I hadn't met any suitable partners. In fact I could think of a dozen or more women who had shown a generous interest in me over the years, both Anglo and Melanesian. But I'd never felt ready to commit to a serious and long-term relationship in accordance with my Christian values of marriage.

Back in my unit in Sydney, I couldn't envisage sitting idle for a month, though I'd take some time to go walking on the beach and enjoy some of the local cafés nearby. I decided that a worthwhile holiday project would be to reupholster grandfather's rosewood chair. It was to be a labour of love and no expense spared to restore it to pristine condition again. I'd maintained a small one-bedroom unit in Narrabeen, on the northern beaches of Sydney. I especially liked it because it included a generous lockable garage that gave me room for a workshop and storage space.

The crate wasn't heavy, though large enough to be a little clumsy to manhandle alone. But I managed. Removing the top and two sides gave me good access to the chair. Once again I was able to marvel at its character and craftsmanship.

The timber needed to be revived and I'd purchased some quality furniture oil to rub in with a soft cloth. The armrests on the other hand had become shiny, especially at the extremities. I could picture my grandfather fondly stroking the rosewood, his calloused fingers feeling for the grain and groove of the carvings. I'd use a cleaning agent to first of all remove the coating of grease and sweat from the armrests before applying the oil.

I must have spent over an hour just roaming over the chair with my eyes, taking in some of its character and features, imagining the craftsman at work. As I familiarised myself better with the carvings I noted a few small chips missing here and there, but otherwise they were in good shape. A crocodile intertwined with a snake, a tribal mask, and what looked like a dog's foot carved into each leg of the chair.

One shape mystified me though. The upper part of each front leg, immediately below the armrests, was something that looked like a couple of upside-down cupcakes on top of each other. These seemed to almost be the intentional focus of attention, enhanced by their prominent position at the front of the chair. Was their position also symbolic, placed just under the hand of the person seated? What actually did these shapes represent?

My curiosity about the aesthetics of the chair satisfied for the moment, I considered how to reupholster the fabric cushion. The underside of the cushion had been neatly bordered with fancy headed tacks. Even the underside reflected exquisite workmanship. Removing these tacks, which I'd need to do carefully to avoid damaging the timber, should release the cushion cover.

Dislodging the tacks proved easier than I first thought, but what awaited me was more of a surprise. With the cover material pulled back on three sides, a delicately made rosewood pocket carefully lodged into the frame of the chair was revealed. After a few minutes of experimenting to find a way to dislodge the pocket, I managed to slide it sideways slightly, and it separated from the chair. A very clever design had allowed this timber seclusion to remain secure and concealed in the chair for decades.

But my surprise was complete when out of the pocket slid a book.

It was old and well worn, in fact very well worn, to the extent of being tattered at the corners. Bound in typical old-style bookbinding, the cover was a faded green swirl, with brown leather triangular corners. The spine was of similar brown leather. There was no notation evident anywhere on the cover or spine.

Cautiously I began to open the book, careful in case the binding failed and loose pages fell out. It was sturdy enough though, and contained two tattered ribbons to mark significant pages.

As I slowly turned the pages, I became aware of a sense of awe and wonder that enveloped me the longer this book rested in my hands. It didn't contain any typeset printing. Instead every page radiated the deep aura of copperplate handwriting in ink or pencil. It could only be the most personal life reflections of an unknown author, but one whose meticulous cursive was matched by the craftsmanship of the chair itself. Could they in fact be one and the same person?

The pages were a little discoloured in places but in remarkable condition. I wondered if the rosewood storage pocket had provided a natural shield from moisture and bugs. My sightseeing journey like a new tourist through its pages completed, I returned to visit the first pages in detail, hopefully to discover the author.

On the inside cover, in perfect copperplate, I read,

"The Diary of Luigi Orlando Giazano".

My grandfather.

The chair restoration consumed me for the rest of my holiday, though I did find time to start reading the first few pages of the diary. I couldn't match the cushion material but found a tapestry style material that was close. The chair still maintained its character and charm but bristled with class. I decided then that I needed to take it back to PNG with me.

Chapter 6

The Journey

It soon became apparent to me that my grandfather's diary was no less than the story of his own adventure to Papua New Guinea nearly eighty years earlier. While I knew that he'd visited PNG as a young man, very little had ever been said about this within my family. It wasn't that it was taboo; rather that it was ancient family history that none of the modern generation showed much interest in.

As I started to read, I became entranced by his experience, recanted in the manner of a true storyteller.

"…. 1922. Boarded the vessel SS Morinda in Brisbane Port. The vessel is operated by Burns Philp & Co, and used for passengers and cargo throughout the Pacific Islands. At 260' length and 1971 tons gross weight, she appears seaworthy enough. I am glad to finally board after waiting for several months for a vessel due to the rat plague that has stopped shipping on the east coast to New Guinea. I was allocated quarters to the aft of the vessel, on the starboard side with a brass rimmed porthole which I find I can open with some difficulty. The slight breeze it affords is welcome in the otherwise cramped and rather stuffy quarters…."

He continued for several pages to recall glimpses of the living conditions on the ship before turning to comment on some of the other passengers he sailed with.

"I find myself quite attentive to the stories of some of the other passengers, and extremely interested to discover their own reasons for travel. Among them is a colleague of a Mr Hurley, adventurer and photographer, who is mounting an extraordinary expedition into the wilderness of New Guinea. Apparently Mr Hurley plans to utilize several aircraft and his colleague describes the same machines in detail. The first has been shipped to Port Moresby in a previous sailing and is being prepared for his arrival.

"The Curtiss Seagull as it is called sounds a remarkable vehicle, resembling a speedboat with two wings and single engine mounted above the pilots. Mr Hurley envisages flying to the remotest regions of the island by flying round the coast and up the rivers. Another aircraft called a Shrimp will provide a back up.

"Indeed, the more I converse with the gentleman, and listen with acquired interest to his accounts of Mr Hurley's escapades, the more I realize that he is no less than a remarkable pioneer in his field."

Grandfather continued to journal about his trip to PNG. His keen eyes and ears for detail amazed me. This gift of observation and his journalistic skills would keep me riveted to the pages of his diary for a long time. I looked forward to his observations on the country and people whom I now thought I knew so well.

One question had intrigued me. Why had grandfather set sail for PNG in the first instance? What challenge called him to this adventure? Perhaps he thought it was irrelevant to record the reason, or perhaps he thought any reader would understand already. So as I read I looked for clues that might answer my question. There were none. He seemed to delight in writing only of the immediate, the daily chores of sea life and the development of his relationships with the crew and passengers on the ship.

The sea trip was to take over a week, sailing up the coast of Queensland, navigating the safe channels that wound through the Great Barrier Reef, and then across the Gulf of Papua to Port Moresby. What a journey, a far cry from the three-hour jet flight I now enjoyed. But in those days the time taken to travel was useful time - time to read, journal, make plans and preparations, and make friends. Grandfather obviously relished all those activities. So as the prospect of a landing at Port Moresby drew closer, I began to see him starting to reflect on his own plans – and the reason for his journey.

"It is the third day since we last saw any semblance of mainland, if a small coconut studded tropical island on the Great Barrier Reef can be described as mainland. The vastness of the ocean surrounds us, its eternal horizon unreachable, yet walling us in on all sides. We cannot escape. Whatever way we turn, it is a wall of water, the horizon like a fence we cannot scale, always there, never diminishing, never getting any closer, never getting any further away.

"But this afternoon we got our first glimpse of hope. In the distance clouds billowed into the heavens, massive thunderstorm clouds reflecting yellow like gold as they caught the rays of the setting sun across the western sea. The Skipper has told us stories of these tropical afternoon storms that build up on the mountain ranges that arch along the spine of the island. The heat can be oppressive enough to set your head aching until the clouds burst and send torrents of water to the earth. Surely the golden skies must also reflect a golden earth – will the rivers of rain also lead me to the rivers of gold?"

At last I had my answer - it was the lure of gold that drew my grandfather like a magnet to New Guinea!

I'd read a little about those gold rush days but even a casual glance into the history of PNG is speckled with gold dust. The country owes much of its early pioneering development to these gold prospectors. Remote areas were pioneered and opened up by prospectors who braved incredibly difficult conditions to find their fortune. Those pioneers of the 1920's gave way to the entrepreneurs of the 1930's and beyond, and the establishment of huge mining and processing plants at places like Wau and Bulolo.

Aviation in PNG really traces its origins to the demand for aircraft to meet the transportation needs of these mining ventures. Airstrips were carved out of the jungle and the feats of early aviation pioneers are legendary as they flew their underpowered fabric covered aircraft in and out of these jungle strips. Larger aircraft such as the Junkers and Ford Trimotor were imported and carried huge loads from Lae into the mining camps. Such was the demand for airfreight that at times in the 1930s more airfreight was carried on aircraft into the hinterlands of PNG than in the rest of the world. Mr Hurley had little idea how much his Seagull, the first aircraft to fly in PNG, would pave the way for the future.

Prospecting camps were rugged places, often accessible only by days and days of trekking. Jungle pathways were soaked with rain and swollen with leaches. Conditions were stark. Prospectors lived under little more than canvas tents propped up by bush cut timbers and relied on vegetable and meat supplies bargained from the local villagers. Some of these were certainly not found on menus in their homeland! Malaria proved to be a real problem, just as living in continually damp conditions rotted the clothes on their back and leather round their feet, and then depleted their mind of hope.

I wondered what grandfather had in mind as he prepared to disembark in Port Moresby? I continued to read.

"As the morning sun rises, we see the outline of mountains in the north. The storm clouds have vanished, the sky is crystal clear and blue, and the peaks of mountain ranges rise majestically, as if proclaiming victory over the storms. These mountains must be much higher than any in

Australia, but has anyone climbed them and measured them yet? We should disembark early this afternoon."

His words may have been more prophetic than he realised. He probably had his sights on Mt Victoria, just to the north west of what was to become the famous WWII Kokoda Track.

"As I prepare to leave my cramped cabin and find my land legs again, I have been able to review my equipment and belongings in preparation for my plans once we arrive. I am told that some supplies are available in Port Moresby but that it is better to bring as much of what is considered essential to one's own mission. The cost of goods in Port Moresby is likely to be high given the freight charges as well as the ample commission demanded by retailers, the most successful of whom are of Chinese origin I am told.

"My clothing is limited to three pairs of trousers that will weather well, a number of shirts both short and long sleeved, and two felt hats. I believe the weather conditions can cause more rapid deterioration than I expect. I have also stocked an extra pair of leather walking boots. My panning equipment is basic so that I am not burdened with carrying a large weight when hiking, though I expect that I will need to engage the services of several local men to assist as carriers with tent gear and food supplies.

"Overall though I am well pleased with the way I have been able to condense my belongings into easily transportable containers. Mr Hurley's friend has been invaluable in his advice about preparing for expeditions into the hinterlands."

My grandfather's plan was becoming clearer by the paragraph. He intended to prospect for gold.

Chapter 7

The Return

My second request of Kila was to spend a month at Mambusu village in the midst of the Moiamba people of Namel Province in order to understand the situation on the ground there. The visit would also pre-empt the Warden's meetings that I'd conduct there in the near future. This was the first time I'd actually taken the opportunity to seriously consider how a mine would affect the local people by spending time in their area, getting to know them first. From Kila's perspective, getting the project right was essential, so he had no qualms about my request.

Despite my two decades in PNG, I'd not actually returned to Mambusu since the rugby game that started my PNG adventure some twenty-six years earlier. It's not that I tried to stay away but the circumstances that would allow me the time to travel up there never presented. At least that was my excuse. In reality I realized I'd just allowed myself to become so busy that I'd procrastinated on returning. Until now.

It was still a reasonable drive, taking several hours. The road was bitumen all the way. This time I was in the comfort of a government issued, air conditioned 4WD Toyota Hilux twin cab. The road took the same route, not that I could remember much of it after all these years. The bends as it snaked up the mountainsides were the same even if the dust was not.

The village had grown considerably since 1972. It was now almost a small town, though maintained the character of a village. That was mainly because of its primary ethnic Moiaimba population, where everyone knows each other and most people are related. The local progress association ran a guesthouse and my secretary had booked accommodation there ahead of time by telephone.

"You're very lucky to get through on the phone," she was told by the receptionist. She'd requested a room with ensuite bathroom for the four weeks I'd be there. Unfortunately, there was only a common bathroom for all guest rooms.

I must admit to deep feelings of both excitement and apprehension as I set out from Port Moresby mid morning. Returning to the place where it all started had a sort of fairy tale feeling to it, yet what would I find? Would the reality of my teenage remembrances be shattered by the stark reality of a now urbanized community? From my experience around PNG I knew that there were few, if any, towns now that did not experience major social issues ranging from alcohol overload to youth gangs. Growing settlement and squatter fringe communities who usually bore the brunt of accusations of crime.

What sort of reception would I find now? Would anyone remember me after all these years? Would I recognise anyone or anything there?

The drive seemed to take forever yet the time passed quickly as my mind raced through my many questions, intermingled with distant memories of my first visit. I found myself driving slower than normal in the last few kilometers as I approached the village, wondering what this revisit would find, savouring the excitement of the unknown. What new adventure may I be getting myself into now?

The last bends into Mambusu seemed familiar, though it was probably just in my mind. Then there it was, the last hill. As I rounded the last corner, the village emerged over the hill as I slowly, almost majestically, drove in and parked outside the local guesthouse. *Mambusu Guest Haus*, the sign read. The paint was flaking but the words gouged into the wooden sign would remain for years to come. There was no welcoming committee, no fanfare, no *leis* around my neck, just a few locals strolling around the street and some children playing nearby.

Ah, incognito. At last. I was a nobody, just passing through. That's how I wanted it.

I recognised the school building, both aged and modified. The old village square where we sat round a fire and watched *singsings* was now a street, part bitumen and part pothole. Permanent material buildings now lined each side of the road, some timber, some fibro, some painted, some not. Some were business premises, some residential. Some both.

Behind and beside these I could see numerous settlement houses made of bits of plywood, tin, corrugated iron, blue tarpaulin and bush timber. Throughout PNG urban growth has been so rapid that the creation of infrastructure has had no hope of maintaining the pace required to support it. Most towns now had squatter settlement populations both within and shrouding their outskirts.

Mambusu only mirrored the national trend as more and more people moved from their villages into the town – probably in the hope of work and a better future. Some had received an education in the town and found it too hard now to move back to the village. This settlement population at Mambusu may have been no more than several hundred people, but it was in microcosm what the larger towns were now experiencing.

I grabbed my bags and entered the Guest Haus, noting as I climbed the timber staircase to the verandah that this building was also in need of repair. Behind a desk in one corner of the foyer was a young local woman who greeted me, obviously awaiting my arrival.

"Hello, welcome to Mambusu. Are you Mr Orlando?" she asked in perfect English.

I nodded and replied. It was nice now to have one person at least know who I was and be expecting my arrival. She introduced herself as Lily and offered any assistance I needed during my stay.

This was a strange situation for me though. As a senior public servant I was used to having an entourage of people welcome and look after me when I visited different places. In the course of my duties it was in the best interests of both the mining companies and the local community to ensure that I was well catered for. That way both groups could ensure I was working in their best interests. Or should I say, that I had no reason not to work for both of their best interests. I realized that I'd tried to keep this visit as low key as possible, including not allowing my Secretary to state my job position. How strange it felt to not have the kind of fanfare I had become used to.

The receptionist interrupted my thoughts. "I'll show you to your room Mr Orlando, it's number 12." I thought she sounded better educated than I would expect a receptionist in the middle of nowhere to be.

The walls of the Foyer and Reception area were decorated with carvings and artifacts that I presumed were from the local area, though some were from regions I knew better. A Sepik crocodile. A Manus garamut. An Oro tapacloth. I followed her down a rather plain corridor until we came to Room 12, and Lily opened the door and ushered me in.

"We're so glad that you've come here," she said with surprising sincerity and warmth, as if she knew something more than her words revealed. "We hope you enjoy your stay. Just contact me if you need anything."

I had some basic questions, such as where the dining room and bathroom was, but these could wait. So also, could the questions I had about how I could achieve the things I wanted to do here – quality time to spend with the leaders and community, learning some of their ways and understanding how a gold mine would really affect them and their environment.

First, I needed a cup of tea after the drive. Fortunately, the Mambusu Guest Haus did provide a hot water jug and tea bags, and did have running water, mostly cold, and electricity. As I sat on the edge of what was to be my bed for the next four weeks, I realized that the trip up had been more tiresome than I'd expected. That was probably a result of all the emotional stuff it involved for me as much as the actual drive.

I woke with a start. Someone was banging on the door. It took a few seconds to register where I was and then recognise Lily's voice.

"Mr Orlando, are you there? Some people have come to see you," she called.

Staggering to my feet I opened the door.

"I'm sorry to disturb you Mr Orlando. The village leaders are here to welcome you. They're in the main room waiting for you."

"Oh, thank you Lily, I'll be out in a minute," I managed, not knowing quite what time it was or how long I had slept. I found my watch on the bedside table. It was a good three hours later than I last remembered, and it was evening.

The 'main room' as Lily called it was in fact also the Dining Room with some well-worn lounge chairs in one corner. As I approached, a small group of men rose from their seats to greet me in Tok Pisin, accompanied by their traditional PNG handshake. I'd learnt it earlier as I prepared for this visit. After shaking hands, each person squeezes their middle finger and thumb against the other person's fingers. The result is a finger snap as they separate, the louder the better, and the handshake is completed. Their awareness that I already spoke Tok Pisin was ample evidence that they were also well aware of who I was. The way in which I naturally slid into their handshake would have confirmed it. Did I really think I could sneak in the back door?

"Welkam tru long ples bilong mipela ol Moiaimba lain" (welcome to the home of the Moiaimba people). Lily came forward with a *lei* and dropped it over my head as I stooped for the occasion. The aroma of freshly picked frangipani flowers tickled my nose as it slid over my head. The sensual feel of the fresh flowers as Lily lowered the floral necklace onto my chest seemed out of character with the tattered chairs and stares of hardwood carvings on the wall. A hint that beneath the tough cultural exteriors lay a softness, a grace, that forged relationships and extended friendships.

"We're very honoured to have you come and visit us and want your stay to be a very memorable occasion for you," the man, who I presumed was the leader of the group, continued. His English, which he now spoke in, was excellent.

Formalities over, I motioned for the group to sit.

The members of the welcoming group introduced themselves to me one by one. Time was not of importance and no one measured it. The spokesman for the group was, as I had thought, the village leader or headman. The strength of his grip and warmth of his welcome surprised me. Little else gave away his position of authority except perhaps an old *lului's* badge. Pinned awkwardly on the left hand side of his fading blue shirt, it was a relic of the colonial administration. He didn't seem that old. I wondered if it was his father's? Perhaps I would ask one day. He introduced himself as Umbare David, a name that seemed familiar but somehow still obscure.

The other members of the group included the local Council President, John Aitomo; the Head Teacher of the school, Paul Wondango; a representative of the local business community, Hendros Kipa; and a softly spoken representative of the local Member of Parliament whose name I could not catch.

So, this was how the next chapter in my journey with the Moiaimba people would begin.

Chapter 8

The Lakatoi

The meeting was brief. I'd been officially welcomed and the leaders showed no desire to stay any longer. We'd have plenty of time to talk together over the next few weeks. So, after a meal in the dining room, I took the opportunity to stay in the lounge and continue reading grandfather's diary.

"Port Moresby harbour is magnificent, a marvel in construction by the hand of a benevolent Creator, a master designer and sculptor. The coastline is guarded by shallow coral reefs but a passage through has been found which allows easy entrance for even the deepest vessels. Entering the harbour one has no inclination as to the size and extent of its grandeur.

"Almost treeless hills surround all sides providing shelter from the prevailing winds, depending on the location within selected by the Captain. This magnificent harbour must be at least 5 miles in length and some 2 miles in breadth and could accommodate hundreds of vessels if called upon to do so.

"As we approached the harbour, native vessels drew near to us. Dugout canoes with up to a dozen bronzed paddlers, all men, tried to come alongside and with ferocious paddling, maintain their pace with ours. Almost naked, the paddlers were adorned with necklaces that tailed down their glistening bare backs. Some sported large frizzy hairstyles decorated with feathers. One canoe came into close enough proximity for me to gain a better

perspective on the natives' attire. The necklace tails were actually large beaks, which I am advised is from native hornbills.

"In the distance we could see much larger sailing craft, outrigger vessels with huge triangular sails. Our arrival had obviously caused a commotion in the community. As we sailed towards the wharf, surrounded now by canoes and brown faces, I noticed that the harbour was lined, at least near the wharf location, with villages.

"It was the style of houses that caught my attention. Built actually over the water, the bush material houses rode on the calm water of the harbour like spiders, their spindly legs thrust down into the sea. What a beautiful spectre it created. Already this harbour and its people have captured my imagination and I have not yet disembarked from the ship!"

The words of Luigi Giazano, my grandfather, were captivating. As I read on, I found myself thrust back in time to my own arrival in Port Moresby, so different in an age of technology and jet travel. Yet I could imagine the excitement, the raw emotion and sense of awe and wonder that he wrote of as he saw the landscape of PNG for the first time, enthralled by the customs and culture of these people. I felt like I was reliving my own experience.

A bond was forming, a bond far greater than familial ties with an ancestral spirit. Something quite ethereal. A bond that somehow seemed to be transporting each of us into the other's world.

"Docking at the timber wharf was routine though the brown bodies working up and down the wharf, in and out of the ship, like ants with goods on their shoulders, provided a sight. It appears that while we may use more sophisticated mechanisms for unloading our vessels, the abundance of native labour here provides a much more effective means of disembarkment. It is a wonderful sight of activity and productiveness, albeit in the stifling heat and humidity.

"Port Moresby itself is simple. Government administrative buildings dot the small hills that surround the bay, all within an hours walking distance. Trading stores have sprung up here and there and one gets the impression that there is a rapidly growing interest in this land. Gold fever perhaps!

"Amongst the Administration buildings of the Australian Government a church or two is also visible. Unexplored lands and adventure draw the young government patrol officer. Unspent dollars draw the shrewd Chinese businessman. Gold dust draws the wishful entrepreneur. And lost native souls draw the missionary. What an odd collection of people we have here! Surely a mystery writer would have a field day with such a cast.

"Once I had collected my baggage and arranged carriers, I found my way from the wharf along the dirt road and up over the peninsula to the southeast, to a guest house which faced Ela Beach. Just over a small but steep hill, it was a different world. A long white sand beach stretches from the headland of the peninsula to another spider like village on the water, called Koki. The wind, which I had barely noticed from within the harbour, was quite evident now, blowing a good 20 miles an hour from the southeast, almost right into Ela Beach. The value of the harbour was even more appreciated. Trying to dock in a wind like this would be quite difficult, though once on the water, it was a beautiful breeze for sailing craft."

Grandfather continued his diary over the next few days with descriptions of Port Moresby, introducing me to this picturesque early colonial settlement. I was fascinated with his travels as he explored the quarters and backwaters of the place.

At Hanuabada, the harbour village on stilts, he quickly made some friends whom he engaged to teach him the local language, Hiri Motu. He soon discovered that Hanuabada means "big village". He was proving to have not only a keen eye for observing people but also a keen ear and tongue for language learning. It seems that in a matter of days he was able to engage in basic conversation in Hiri Motu. Reading between the lines I observed that his ability to make friends with the locals was soon legendary in the community.

To the southeast he found Koki village to be a source of fresh seafood, with reef fish and crustaceans readily available for bargains of matches, mirrors or even a knife. I began to see a trend in his writings. While descriptions of landscape and scenery were plentiful, his real focus was the people. And so, in every paragraph the spotlight of his writing and description became people. Sometimes a group of dancers, sometimes a child, sometimes a family or clan, other times a mother or father, son or daughter. His insights into their customs began to shine past his descriptions of their physical appearance. He was no less than an amateur social anthropologist having a field day.

"After three weeks in the humid tropical atmosphere of Port Moresby I depart today for the hinterland further along the Papuan coast, in search of gold. I have heard that there are vast valleys which are unexplored but which have yielded significant quantities of gold from panning in the coastal mouths of their rivers. Like fishermen boasting of the one that got away, the stories are sometimes wild and beyond imagination. But I have seen some of the gold brought in by the occasional prospector. Beautiful and sparkling, the dust of heaven!

"I obtained the services of some natives with whom I had built up a friendship to take me along the coast in one of their coastal trading vessels, an outrigger called a lakatoi. Magnificent sailing vessels with long outrigger poles and bark cloth triangular sails. Hulls carved from hollowed out tree trunks, with enough room on the sliced palm decking to accommodate a family. Depending on the season and winds, the Motuan people sail up and down the coast trading various goods, especially shells and salt, for things they cannot otherwise procure. These include specific ochres, animal bones and exotic feathers, used in their traditional ceremonial costumes. They describe trading ports

along the coast with trading trails stretching right into the mountains, transversing the animosity between rival tribes.”

I turned to the next page.

“It is on one of these trading trips that I am now a passenger. What a fascinating journey this is proving to be! The sheer size of this vessel is admirable. The bush material shelter on the deck is like a small house, complete even with a fireplace for cooking. Traditional clay pots are used to house food and some take their place as cooking vessels. Fresh fish are abundant as my newfound friends spear anything edible within range that dares to even blink at them.

“What is amazing is their sailing and navigational skills. Without map or compass they seem to know the currents and winds and ocean depth as if it were their own childhood playground. For mile after mile we sail just off the coast but never have I observed any hesitation by the helmsman as he craftily guides the vessel, even at night. Dressed only in a bark cloth wrapped from front to back around a vine belt, like a sumo wrestler's loincloth, his fine brown muscular torso glistens from the salt spray occasionally thrown up by the sea. Iri has become a good friend in the last few days as we prepared for and commenced this voyage. Despite my halting rendition of his Motu language, he has warm-heartedly welcomed me along. His explanations of traditional seafaring and fishing are taking me into a new world of seeing alternatives and new modes of viewing the world. Why do we westernised people think that we know everything?

“It was a pleasure to meet Iri's family, who joined us on the trip. His wife Konio graced me with a wonderful abundance of food while Iri described to me the various fish and crustaceans she had prepared. His three beautiful children are a delight to them both. I marveled at how lovingly Iri held his small son in his arms for hours, both enjoying the tactile contact so essential to bonding. To be sitting under a shelter on a lakatoi with a fire in the middle of the floor, eating traditional seafood delicacies with a bare

breasted mother, half naked husband and their naked children, is a picture I will never forget."

....

"The sun is hot and the humidity high, my constant state of perspiration is not helped by the salt spray. My host family on the lakatoi is gracious and ensures that I have shade under the shelter. There is no privacy as such, we sleep huddled together on the deck. Ablutions are conducted discreetly at one end of the vessel where access to the sea is easy. But I am learning that privacy for these communal people is not needed. It is a foreign concept. They have each other and daily provision of food by nature, and that is all they need."

....

"After three days of sailing, we sail closer to the shore until Iri finds a small inlet and sails into it. He advises me that this is where the trading track up to the mountain areas commences. My carriers have come on a second vessel and dock close behind. I am definitely glad to get onto dry land again but will need a few hours of rest to get my land legs. To my surprise Konio gives me a supply of food, taro and dried fish, wrapped in a bag woven from pandanas leaves. Their generosity is unparalleled. Tonight I will allow the carriers to enjoy a good meal while we camp here to sort out the packs and prepare for our trek inland in search of gold."

In my mind's eye I had been tracing grandfather's track along the coast, past the various inlets. They had become familiar to me from years of window gazing as a passenger on Air Niugini F27 and F28's as they traced their pathway out of Port Moresby. I thought that perhaps I would try and retrace his seaward journey one day.

But for now, as I sat reading in the lounge at the Mambusu Guest Haus, there was a growing sense of excitement as he prepared to travel inland. I recalled the point at which the road from Port Moresby to Mambusu left the coast and headed for the mountains, following the Moi River. Where exactly was grandfather headed inland?

It was getting late in the evening. Lily had switched the main lights out, leaving me a light for reading.

"Excuse me, Mr Orlando", she politely reminded me, "don't forget that our generator goes off at 10 o'clock, and if the town power is off, you'll be in darkness".

I acknowledged, knowing that I should have been heading for bed, but I needed to know where it was that grandfather was going, if his diary would give me any clue soon.

"The inlet we landed at is actually the final small delta of a river that has its headwaters thousands of feet above us. After a humid night with marauding sand flies and mosquitoes, I woke to a beautiful clear morning. There was a touch of dew on the tent canvas but it soon dried out as the sun rose over the mountains to the north east of us.

"The majestic outline of these ranges holds me in suspense. Perhaps only 30 or 40 miles away, the rugged peaks silhouetted against the rising sun are, I know, deceptive in their beauty. The many stories of ventures into these mountains that I heard while in Port Moresby make me realize that the unprepared will pay the price for their unpreparedness. Their beauty is obviously matched by their ability to reduce grown men to miserable wretches in a matter of weeks. I have done all I can to prepare as best I can, and trust that God will bear me up for what I cannot prepare for".

The light went out and I was in darkness. I found myself unprepared!

As I stumbled my way down the guest haus corridor to try and find my room in the dark, I tried to recall whether Room No 12 was on the left or right side of the corridor, and how far down it was.

I found a door that I thought was mine and fumbled with the key. It didn't work and I realized I might be terrorizing another guest who thinks someone is breaking into his or her room. I prepared myself to call out an apology, or perhaps confront a sleepy but angry guest, but nothing. So I felt my way down to the next door and the key fitted. By the time I'd kicked my shins against the bed frame and knocked over a bed lamp, I'd found my torch.

My shins were aching as I rolled into bed, but that was nothing compared to the intrigue of not knowing which river grandfather was following.

Chapter 9

The Welcome

The quietness at night at Mambusu was almost deafening. I realized I'd grown used to the noises of city life in Port Moresby. When I awoke it was already quite light outside. A quick peek through my single louvered window revealed nothing but opaque white mist. Highland's mornings. I loved them.

Something was wrong though. My book was gone.

Grandfather's precious diary was no longer on my bedside table and my heart was in panic. Had someone come into my room and taken it? Then I remembered the closing events of last night. I must have left it in the lounge room when the lights went out.

I still hadn't registered what time it was but quickly got myself dressed enough to duck out to the lounge hopefully without being seen by any of other guests. The diary was next to the chair I'd been sitting in but to my surprise it was open at a different page than I'd been reading, as if someone else had begun to read it as well.

Not wanting to waste time to solve that mystery, I picked it up and was just turning around to leave when a voice came from behind me.

"Good morning Mr Orlando". It was Lily.

"Good morning Lily", I replied, feeling a little embarrassed, "I must've left my book here last night... the lights went out on me".

"I thought so. The book you were reading looks very interesting", she responded, inviting conversation. Was she hinting that she had also been reading it?

"Yes, it's very old and part of my family history. Did you see it before I came in?" I was starting to feel a little threatened thinking that Lily might have let herself into my own very private world. That made me feel a bit defensive.

Lily was apologetic. "Oh, I'm sorry Mr Orlando, I was just sweeping the floor in the morning and found it lying on the floor. The handwriting is so beautiful I couldn't resist looking at it."

I relaxed. "Thank you for picking it up then, I appreciate you doing that. It's actually a diary written by my grandfather. It was given to me recently. No one in our family knew about it."

"Did you know him?" asked Lily, obviously keen to keep the conversation going.

"A little. He was a really kind old man who passed away soon after I finished my university studies. He was nearly 90 and lived by himself. His wife had died many years earlier so I never knew her. I would visit him every now and then but he never said anything about his diary. It was hidden in an old chair he passed on to me after he died."

Lily listened but didn't reply. Maybe my answer didn't make sense? It seemed right to ask of her family.

"What about your family Lily, are they here in Mambusu?" I asked.

"Yes, but my mother and father have both died. We were living in Port Moresby and they were in a PMV which had a bad accident." She paused for a brief moment, as if determined not to relive that time again, and continued. "I've got two brothers and a sister. They're in Port Moresby still living with my aunty at Gerehu. My sister's at school and my brothers are at university at Waigani."

"I'm sorry to hear of your parent's accident. Is this your home village then? Is that why you're here by yourself and not in Port Moresby?" I asked.

"Yes, that's part of it. I wanted to come back home to my village. But there's something else. I felt that God was calling me back here for some important reason that I can't explain. Maybe one day I'll understand?"

I was enjoying this discussion with Lily and intrigued as she opened up to me so quickly about this mystery in her life, the mystery of her return to Mambusu.

As we talked, I began to study her face and found myself admiring her eyes. They were so alive and so expressive. Her rich brown complexion and wavy dark hair tied up in a ribbon at the back of her head was typical of many PNG women, but her eyes captivated me. I was beginning to consider that there was far more to Lily than just being a receptionist at this Guest Haus.

There were voices and a door opened.

"The leaders are coming to see you now Mr Orlando", Lily advised me matter of factly, and then turned on her heels and left.

I suddenly realized that it was nearly 10 am, and I still hadn't had breakfast. Quick as I could I raced back to my room and got ready to meet the leaders again. I remembered that after a brief introduction last night they advised they'd meet me this morning. *Maski* breakfast, a cup of tea would have to do!

I didn't keep them waiting more than a few minutes, guessing that Lily would let them know I was on the way. They rose as I entered the room and in typical PNG fashion, warmly shook hands and clicked fingers. Whatever hope I had that I was an unknown had disappeared. They were well aware of who I was, and what my work was. It was now time for business.

"Mr Orlando, while we welcome you warmly to Mambusu, we'd like to know why you are visiting? This isn't a place visited by tourists or for holidays by people like you. We'd like to know what your business here is?" The question was asked directly and matter of factly by Umbare David, who had earlier introduced himself as a senior village leader.

"Mr David and gentlemen," I addressed them with respect, "I want to assure you that I don't have any hidden agendas in coming to Mambusu and am very happy to tell you the reasons."

I'd considered telling them straight away about my visit to Mambusu all those years ago playing rugby, but for some reason decided to keep that to myself. Perhaps I wanted something up my sleeve in case I needed an ace later on, something that might get me out of trouble if it arose in future?

"As you know I work for the Department of Social Resources. My job is to meet with landowner groups when mining exploration is planned in an area, and to discuss with them the future of their place. I try to provide an understanding of what might occur, and how the government will be involved to help the people find the best financial benefits in their negotiation with mining companies. I've been doing this for over ten years now and …"

"Mr Orlando," interrupted Umbare David, "we're very aware of what you do and your work as a Mining Warden. We have *wantoks* who work in your department and know you. One of your department secretaries is married to my cousin brother's son. So, we knew about you coming."

There was no hiding place for me in this conversation. At least they were keen to get to the point quickly and I appreciated their candour.

Umbare David continued, "What we want to know is *why* you are here now."

"Have you heard of the Namel Mining proposal?" I asked, getting straight to the point with them.

"We've heard that there is interest in the gold in our river, but that has been since white men first came into our area, when my grandfather was a young man", replied Umbare, a faint look of confusion spreading across his face. "Are you saying there is more than that?"

"Brother, there must be", interjected Hendros Kipa, the local businessman. "Do you remember when the Member visited three weeks ago and was very interested in walking down to the river? He didn't say much though." I noted that the Member of Parliament's representative was not actually with the group this morning.

Local Council President John Aitomo had not missed much either. "More than that, he was also asking about leasing land in the village", he said.

"It's true that there is now a proposal by a company to mine and extract gold here," I continued. "I'm here because I wanted to spend some time to assess what the impact of that proposal will have on your community. It is called the Namel Mining Proposal."

There was silence for some minutes as the leaders of Mambusu considered my announcement. It was clear that it was news to them. It was also clear that their Member of Parliament knew but had withheld that information from them. That could only be on the basis that he was planning to make his own pot of gold from the proposal. That idea probably held their thoughts more than the fact of a gold mine in their backyard.

The sound of a door opening startled the group, and the Member's representative entered, apologizing for being late.

"Lily, can you bring us some coffee please," Umbare called out to Lily. His demeanor had suddenly changed, his face now relaxed. "Mr Orlando, we do welcome you here now and so let me tell you a bit about the place so you can enjoy your holiday with us," he continued.

It was obvious that he was changing the course of the conversation and I could see only one reason for that. From now on it would be a political game of survival, to see who got to the gold first!

The rest of the conversation was about the history of the area, some of the beauty spots that I might like to trek to, with some local young men to guide me of course. There was nothing that would seem too hard for Umbare and his team to assist me in enjoying my holiday here. And it was clear that there would be no more mention of gold or gold mining within earshot of the Member's representative!

Chapter 10

The Politician

Lupo Warina was not liked by everyone. That's probably why many people referred to him as "Loopy". Behind his back, of course. But he'd found enough people to like him to vote in his favour at the last two national elections. His seat was the electorate of Moi, which covered the area that was home to the Moiaimba people.

Some people noted that at the time of the elections there was more drunkenness in the electorate, and that Lupo's supporters seemed to be well supplied with beer, and happy to share it. Others noted that some of the more remote villages in the electorate, particularly those that didn't support Lupo, somehow didn't actually receive their ballot papers on voting day and so missed out on casting their votes. There was an outcry about foul play of course, but it never came to a court challenge. So Lupo Warina became the Honourable Lupo Warina MP.

His home village was not Mambusu but a large village called Deria about two kilometers away. There was a rumour that the village was named by early French missionaries who felt it was a backwards place, but nobody really knew. It was accessible once the road had been extended past Mambusu, a project Lupo had spearheaded personally. It was a project that thrust him into the limelight and set him in good standing with most of the community at election time, and so secured his first term in office.

A man with plenty of ambition for his people, Lupo had also learnt that his position of power as a politician allowed him some scope for personal ambition. In fact, with a little bit of shrewdness, he planned to retire from politics as a wealthy man. Some might suggest this was at the expense of his people but he would quickly point out that it was a small price to pay for all the good he had brought to them. He considered it as his entitlement for all that he had done for them.

Others would call it stealing.

The Moiaimba people were well aware that their rivers contained gold. So, it was inevitable that their Member would be the one who would seize the opportunities for the future and begin to look for ways to develop this gold resource. Over the last two years he had quietly made enquiries and built a network of contacts in an effort to realize the gold potential.

Six months earlier, during a governmental visit to several countries in Asia, he had secured an agreement with a South East Asian consortium to move ahead with a gold processing venture. The company had registered itself as Namel Holdings Ltd, with an operating company called Namel Mining Pty Ltd. It was this company that had now officially submitted its proposal to the Minister for Social Resources – the same proposal that had landed on Secretary Kila Woro's desk.

Namel Holdings also spawned some other companies, including one called the Namel Community Trust, which was to receive 15% of dividends from the future gold mine. This was to be a vehicle for disbursement of benefits into the community. In a deal to try and sweeten the acceptability of the project in the local Moiaimba community, the Member for Moi had persuaded the consortium to deposit two million US dollars into the Namel Community Trust account. Chairman of the Board was, of course, Honourable Lupo Warina. This, he assured the consortium, would guarantee quick approval of the project by the community, which would see its benefits immediately.

The Chairman then discretely formed a new company called Moi Futures Ltd as a subsidiary of the Namel Community Trust. This would be the actual vehicle through which Trust funds were capitalized on and distributed. If anyone had checked the IPA company records, they would have discovered that the sole shareholder was registered as Mr L. W. Udio. Udio was Lupo's grandfather's name. The Honourable Lupo Warina MP had successfully established himself a slush fund, and only his closest associates knew that Moi Futures Ltd even existed.

Mr Warina planned to use Moi Futures to lease village owned land that could then be leased back to Namel Mining for their development. This had been foremost in his mind when he visited Mambusu three weeks earlier.

But there was one other thought also in his mind. Mambusu and Deria had been traditional enemies and there was still some rivalry between them. If Moi Futures actually owned a large part of Mambusu land, it would be the ultimate insult for Mambusu - and sweet revenge for Deria!

Chapter 11

The Trap

The day after I arrived at Mambusu, the Member paid a visit to Kila Woro, my boss. Kila was Secretary of the Department of Social Resources, and a man I had worked with and admired for many years.

The visit had been arranged by the Member at a location that provided a bit more privacy than Kila's offices at the Department of Social Resources. Over lunch in a corner table for two at Sandy's Bar & Restaurant in Boroko, the two men discussed progress with the Namel Mining Proposal.

"So how did your trip back to the electorate go, Member?" asked Kila. "Did you get the local support you need?"

"Oh yes, it went really well," lied Lupo, "I didn't find anyone opposing it at all. I had a good look around Mambusu village and there's lots of land available. Went down to the proposed mine site as well near the river and it looks really good. I had good discussions with John Aitomo, LLG President and Hendros Kipa, who has some trade stores there."

"It's a pity you didn't meet up with Justin, who is down there now," said Kila.

"Justin who?" asked Lupo.

"Justin Orlando," replied Kila, realizing that the Member may not know his manager. "He's a manager under me, has done a lot of good work in the initial stages of working with communities in the lead up to exploration and mining projects. He was quite excited about the Namel proposal so I've sent him out for a few weeks to get the people on side."

The Member frowned. "But why do you need him when I'm doing that?" It was almost a command.

"Member, he is out there because he does a good job of this and he makes sure the people are happy with the project. He understands the technical and environmental aspects. He gets everyone on side first," Kila responded.

The Member frowned again. "Is he an expatriate?" he asked.

Kila thought for a few seconds, and then replied, "Well, yes, he's Australian, but he's lived here for more than twenty years. He speaks Tok Pisin like a Sepik, and Motu like a Central."

"So why are we sending out a white foreigner to do the job that I, as Member for that electorate, can do? I represent the government to my people and I'll get them on side. I've told you that already." Lupo recognised he was raising his voice and quickly looked around to make sure no one else in the bar had heard him. No one had, but he lowered his voice anyway and continued.

"Look, why don't we work together on this." Lupo's voice suddenly sounded much more conciliatory, like that of a good friend.

"What do you mean, aren't we already doing that through the department?" queried Kila.

"Yes, but no, I mean we both have interests in seeing this project going ahead. We don't want that jeopardised by this fellow Orlando if he can't get the people on side," said Lupo, fishing for a decent excuse to undermine Kila and his manager.

"I'm not sure I agree with you but keep talking." Kila was suspicious but needed to hear more. "What did you have in mind?"

Lupo, thinking fast, replied, "Ok, you are only a few years off from retiring, and what have you got so far? What's your retirement plans?"

Kila thought for a minute and responded, "You're right, I only want to work for another three years and then retire, go back to Marshall Lagoon and build a nice house for my family."

Lupo saw an opening and surged in. "What about your sons, I know one of them is thinking of getting married as soon as you can get the bride price together. How much are they charging for *meris* these days? Didn't I read in the Post Courier the other day that someone paid 50,000 kina for a girl from Hanuabada?"

"Oh yeah," said Kila, "tell me about it! I know the guy who had to pay it, he's got *dinaus* all over the country now. He'll be in debt till the day he dies!"

It was all Lupo needed. All he had to do now was close the trap.

"So let's say this project is successful, the biggest gold mine in the country. Don't you think the government will reward those who have made it happen? I'll see to that personally." Lupo paused briefly.

"What's your plans for the house?" said Lupo as he threw the conversation back into Kila's hands.

"Well, I've got my land and some rough plans but haven't had the money to buy any timber yet. I guess I'm worried that if I spend money on the house now then I'll find it harder to pay the bride price." Kila had become aware that he was following a lead of conversation that may not be wise, but Lupo had opened the door.

"Ok, let's look at it this way then. I've got some advance funds from Namel Mining to ensure the development can move ahead, and we need to make sure there are no hindrances. So let me have a look at the plans and I'll see what I can do to help," insisted Lupo.

"Look Member, I'm not interested in getting into any illegal practices in this…" Kila quickly responded, only to be cut off by the Member.

"No, no, not at all Kila, neither am I. All I'm saying is that there are funds available to make sure the project is successful, and they can be used at my discretion to make sure that happens." Lupo sounded so convincing. "Of course, this is all above board," he continued quickly, "and the future of my region and our country is at stake. So, tell me about your plans."

As it happened, Kila had been working on a copy of his house plan that morning, and retrieved the penciled paper from his A4 size, Government issue Executive diary.

"Well, I was just working on the plan this morning, doing some estimates," said Kila as he placed the paper in front of the Member and pointed to his calculations. "I reckon that I need about 9,600 kina for the timber. I already have some concrete mix ready to go ahead with the foundations and have nails and tools on site. The block has been cleared for some time. Some *wantoks* helped with that."

Lupo looked over the plans pretending to understand them. He didn't, but Kila was not to know that. After a few minutes he reached into his briefcase and pulled out a chequebook. After writing a cheque, he passed it to Kila.

"Look, here's a contribution to help you buy the timber. It's all above board so just give me the receipt for my records after you buy them." Lupo held the cheque out for Kila to take.

Kila hesitated for a few moments. He was a Christian, a strong United Church man and a respected leader in his congregation. He'd had lots of opportunities to increase his bank account through illegal deals in the past, and had refused. He'd been determined not to participate in corruption.

But today, the way the Member had explained it, the line between good and evil seemed quite blurred. In fact, he was at a loss to see what actually was wrong with the Member choosing to use his funds this way, especially if he would have receipts to properly acquit them. With a small but diminishing tinge of doubt, he reached out and accepted the cheque, which the Member had carefully folded before Kila saw it.

"Bro, I'm so pleased we've been able to work this out together. And just so we're clear, you'll make sure that your man is kept in the dark about my activities, so that he won't get in my way," said Lupo, almost as an aside as he pushed his chair out and walked away.

When the Member had left, Kila discretely unfolded the cheque. It was for 10,000 kina, on the account of Moi Futures Ltd.

Chapter 12

The River

My meeting with the leaders had been short lived due to the revelation of the Member's clandestine activities and the intrusion of his representative. With little else to do, I returned to reading grandfather's diary.

"There is a village near where we camped. My carriers stayed in bush materials shelters built by the villagers, who supplied them some food for which I bargained. They seem to be of the opinion that gold prospectors have gold on their way out to the goldfield as well as on the way back! Be that as it may, I spoke with the villagers and found out that the river is called the Ranu Moi, the Moi River. It is known for its gold sediments. I decided to try for some panning and sure enough, there were some very small traces of dust after an hour of panning. This river will be the one for me."

The Moi River. I let it sink in. This was the same river that flowed from Moiaimba territory down to the sea. The same river that I'd driven beside all those years ago. The same river I could almost hear babbling from the Guest Haus now. I needed to double check and found Lily behind the reception desk.

"Lily, I have a question for you," I said as she looked up from the desk.

"Certainly Mr Orlando, what is it?" Lily replied courteously.

"I just want to confirm that this river that flows down the valley here is called the Moi River," I said.

"Yes, Mr Orlando, this is the Moi River, named after the Moi region here. The name for my people, the Moiaimba, actually means 'the people of the Moi River' in our language."

I thanked her and went back to my reading as calmly as I could. But my heart was pounding now as the threads of my grandfather's journey and my own suddenly became far more entwined. We were both somehow being pulled together by the gold in this river. I could only read on with growing anticipation of what he might have found.

"I had another comfortable night once I had managed to crawl inside my mosquito net. It rained most of the night and the river has come up considerably. I am going to have to travel up beside the river rather than hike up the river itself. The muddy water makes it hard to pan, but the current must be continually washing away at the source of the gold deposits upstream."

Grandfather had his sights clearly on the source of the gold, but whether he would find it I would have to wait and see. I read on as his team set out for the mountains. The first three days were spent on the flat lowlands between the mountains and the coast. The temperature was hot, 34 degrees Centigrade during the middle of the day, and the humidity high, well over 90%.

Mosquitoes and sand flies annoyed, but the leeches drew blood. Grandfather and his crew were constantly ridding themselves of them, trying to get to them before the leeches sunk their teeth in and started to get the taste of human blood. The carriers carried sharpened bamboo that they expertly used like a knife to brush down the side of their leg and flick off any offender. Grandfather knew that lemon juice or salt would make a leech let go, but he had neither to spare so used his own knife, quickly learning the technique from the carriers.

The other danger in the lowlands was snakes. Death Adder, Taipan and Papuan Black were all lurking in the grassy riverbanks, ready to inject their deadly venom if necessary. The Death Adders were a particular concern because they didn't move off the track, and would retaliate only when trodden on. Fortunately they were mostly active at night. The party kept a careful eye out on the path all the time.

It took them three days to reach the foothills of the mountains, and then another four days to reach a place where grandfather felt confident about setting up camp and panning for gold.

"By midday on our seventh day since leaving the coast, we came to a fork in the river. I estimate we are between 2,000 and 3,000 feet in elevation as the air is cooler but still has some humidity. The mountains ahead of us are now starting to tower, and I would estimate they are above 10,000 feet high in places. But even where we are there are steep sided mountains either side of the river, rising up to 5,000 feet and higher. We have kept our journey to the tracks that the natives have made in their journeys to the coast. But at times these are little more than a foot width precipice along the riverbank.

"The river that began as a shallow but wide delta at the coast has become much narrower, now a rock lined, fast flowing river, carved into the sides of the hills. While the terrain is steep right down to the water's edge, it is covered in jungle. As we walk we often hear the cry of exotic birds, and smell exotic animals.

"At one stage there was a musty smell that crept into the air we breathed as we walked. The carriers stopped and had a discussion. There was a kuskus nearby, a native tree possum. Valued for its fur as well as meat, several of the carriers scrambled off into the jungle. The kuskus live high in the trees but their strong aroma gives their position away.

By cutting the tree down, the natives can capture the kuskus. Soon after we heard the clump, clump sound of a tree being put to the axe.

"An hour later the carriers returned with their prize, a spotted kuskus. The animal is beautiful to behold with its round eyes, long tail and lovely fur, a cream colour with brown spots. It is much more attractive than our Australian possums. It was too nice a creature to kill so I redeemed it for a bargain with the carriers. I would keep it as a pet. Some of the carriers made a carrying container of split bamboo tied together with vines lashed to a pole. The kuskus had room to move, but not escape. At least it is still alive!

"There is enough of a flat area in the fork between the rivers for me to establish a camp here. Fortunately, there is no evidence that this area floods. I have seen some glimpses of local native people in the last day's journey to this point and hope to make contact with them soon. They are no doubt watching my every move so I hope they do not perceive me as a threat."

While grandfather was preoccupied with setting up camp, he was also keen to establish relationships with the locals, good relationships that is! His first encounter came the next day.

"At mid morning today I was alerted by the carriers to a group of men coming across the river towards us. The group of a dozen men did not appear to be warriors as such even though dressed only in their scant native clothing. This was little more than a woven string covering wrapped around a vine belt at the front with some large leaves tucked under their belt covering their rear. They carried what looked like hunting spears but as they approached they struck up a dialogue in Motu with the carriers. Little did they know that I also spoke some Motu, but I waited for my time to reveal that secret.

"The men had very occasionally seen white men on the coast, and were surprised to see one come all the way to their location. They were intrigued and wanted to know who

he was and what he was doing here. By this time the men were within earshot of me and so I came forward to stand within three yards of them and introduce myself. Addressing the one who had dialogued in Motu, I told him that my name was Luigi. I was from Australia, a large land across the water to the south. I said that I had seen the gold specks in the river at the coast and wanted to find where they came from. I held out my hand hoping that the tradition of a handshake I had discovered elsewhere also applied here.

"After the spokesman had interpreted my message, the men laughed and laughed, but then held out their hands in greeting. Instead of shaking hands though they hung on and delayed the release as if there was something more our hands should be doing. It was rather strange.

"As for the laughing, I was not aware of what was so funny. But once the men had contained themselves again, the interpreter let me in on the secret.

"'Why, the gold starts here,' he said, pointing just upriver from my camp. 'Everyone knows that!'"

Chapter 13

The Lawyer

That evening as I ate dinner Lily came over to my table to pass me a message.

"Excuse me Mr Orlando," she said politely, "Mr David would like to see you privately tonight. Would he be able to meet you in your room after dinner?"

"Yes, please tell him that I'll wait for him in my room," I replied. I'd wondered when the next meeting would be once the Mambusu men had collected their thoughts.

Just before 8 pm there was a knock on my door and I opened it to find the group of four there, Umbare David, Hendros Kipa, John Aitomo and Paul Wondanga. I ushered them into the room and was about to close the door when I noticed Lily there.

"I'll get some extra chairs, Mr Orlando," she said and was off before I could reply. A half a minute later she appeared with five chairs, obviously placed in readiness just round the corner. As I found my own chair and sat down I noticed that Lily had also now entered the room and had taken a seat with the four others.

Umbare David noticed that I appeared a little surprised that Lily had joined us. "I hope you don't mind Lily joining us as well Mr Orlando. You see, she is a lawyer and Secretary of our Mambusu Progress Association."

I was actually quite glad for Lily's company in the group, and even more so now I was beginning to recognise that her role in the community was far more than just her work as receptionist at the Guest Haus. But that role did give her the ability to listen in on any conversations there. I remembered how she had never been out of earshot at our first meeting.

"I'm delighted to have her join us, Mr David, and also that she's such a valued member of your community. I didn't know she was a lawyer but I know she'll have a big role to play in negotiations between yourselves, the government and mining company."

I looked over at Lily as I spoke. She had a faint but cheeky smile on her face. This had been her little game with me, and she'd won. Game on, I thought!

"I have one condition though, and that is that you gentlemen and Lily call me Justin from now on, not Mr Orlando. Now what can I do for you?" I continued, trying to hide my joy at the way the relationship with these new friends, especially Lily, was developing.

"Namo," said Umbare David, "please call us by own first names as well then, and I prefer just to be called David."

John Aitomo now took on the spokesman role. "Justin, we didn't complete our conversation yesterday. We want you to tell us more about the Namel Mining proposal you asked if we knew about. The answer is no, we've heard nothing about this latest proposal but we think that our Member, Honourable Lupo Warina, has. We knew there was some exploration going on, and some people interested in the gold, but not this proposal. What can you tell us about it?"

I realized that I needed to unpack the proposal sensitively so as not to cause alarm to these community elders, but they were not here to beat around the bush.

"I'll spell it out as simply as I can for you. The government has received a proposal from a South East Asian consortium that wishes to set up a gold extraction plant in the area, and mine the gold and other minerals found here. They believe that this project could become the biggest mine in PNG, and its worth far exceeds Ok Tedi or Bougainville. I've come to spend some time here in order to find out how the Department of Social Resources can work with the community to ensure the best results for the community are achieved. I'm actually doing this in addition to my official role as Warden."

That was most of the truth because my mandate was to get the best results for the government also, but semantics were not so important at this stage.

"I've brought with me the basic plans proposed by the consortium, which has registered as Namel Mining Pty Ltd."

I noticed that Lily had a notepad out and was scribbling notes. No doubt she would be visiting IPA House in Port Moresby very soon to access company records so the group could understand exactly whom they were really dealing with.

"Justin, is there any chance that our Member would not have heard of this? How is it that this has got to the stage of this proposal and we, the community, have not been advised?" asked John.

It was a very valid question, but I needed to be diplomatic in my answer.

"I'm afraid you'll have to ask your Member that question," I responded. "At this stage the Secretary for the Department of Social Resources has engaged me to come here now and make sure that you're well aware of it."

Hendros interrupted me. "When the Member was here a few weeks ago, he asked about leasing land near the river and also in the village, but didn't give any more details. I think he was preparing for this project," he said. "I didn't think much about it at the time but I reckon he had plans and wasn't disclosing them to us. Justin, did you know that our clans from Mambusu and Deria where he comes from are traditional rivals? It makes us nervous."

"There's a lot I don't know about this area," I replied, "but if that's the case, it certainly adds a greater motive for the Member to be wanting to pull the wool over your eyes, as we say."

"Can you explain this proposal to us in detail please Justin?" asked David, regaining his authority again.

"I'd be very happy to David, but can I suggest we do it during the day when there is plenty of time to spread out the diagrams, maps and papers, and you can ask questions. I really want you to understand exactly what is involved, not only for the mine but for the future of your region."

David was keen to find out more as soon as possible. "Well, let's meet tomorrow morning then," he said.

"What about the Member's representative, do we include him?" chipped in Paul the Head Teacher.

The others thought about this for all of two seconds, and were unanimous in their decision that he should be left out of the discussion.

"Until we know what the Member is up to," said David, "we should leave him out. We don't want to be spied on."

"Then we'll need to meet where he won't barge in or find us. Let's meet in my Head Teacher's office at the school at 10 o'clock." I hadn't heard Paul say much before but he was obviously a solution finder, someone who could see through problems. The group would need such a person in future because there'd be many challenges ahead.

"Do you have any comments from a legal perspective, Lily?" I asked her, keen to let her know I appreciated her involvement.

"Well, the Member may be breaching his duty of care to his electorate but I'm not sure yet if he's breaching any laws." Lily was obviously thinking through any legal implications she knew of. "I want to get down to Moresby soon and check the company records to see what I can find out about Namel Mining Pty Ltd. There are sure to be associated companies that may give us more of a clue.

After a pause, Lily continued. "I do find it strange that we don't know much about this proposal. There was a lot of initial exploration done here in the 1970s and 80s. Some of it was quite detailed. I think an Environmental Impact Study was conducted by one of the companies, and I heard talk of social mapping studies but not sure if one was ever completed. I was young enough to not be noticed but old enough to hear and understand what was going on at the Guest Haus. That's when I started working there, as a waitress."

"That history should all be on record then. Perhaps the Member has been at work to rekindle interest in a mine but kept his cards up his sleeve. He might be trying to piggyback on the earlier work done here?" I suggested.

"By the way, what branch of law did you specialize in?" I asked Lily, fully confident in her abilities in company law.

"Oh, yes, family law," she replied. Again, that cheeky smile!

Chapter 14

The Proposal

It was a foggy morning again in Mambusu, even at 10 am, as I walked over to the school to meet the others. I'd spent the rest of the previous day going through the Namel Mining Proposal in detail by myself. I needed to be able to answer their questions accurately. While the details of the plan were on paper, the real impact of this venture on the community was not. This was something I'd have to explore with them in dialogue. For the moment they just wanted to know the plan.

We'd all gathered, except the Member's representative, by 10:10 am. The Proposal's maps and diagrams were on colour A3 sheets, with some plastic bound A4 books about three centimetres thick accompanying them. I took the group through each coloured sheet so they could appreciate the scope and size of the venture.

"At its basic level the company will build a two lane bitumen road from the coast to Mambusu and perhaps even to Deria. It'll follow the same pathway as the current single lane road, but there'll be places where improvements such as shaving off tight corners will be done. There'll be a lot of traffic using this road, including semi-trailers and road trains. The road will improve your transport opportunities but bring its own problems with the volume and size of traffic."

I could see my friends starting to take in the elements of the plan as I explained them, but it was not yet the time for questions.

I continued. "The Proposal appears to build on the work done earlier under various Exploration Licenses in the 1970s and 80s, though some Licenses were renewed into the 90s. So I'm presuming that some of this will be familiar to you even though most of that was over a decade ago. It calls for the main mining operation to be set up down near the river, perhaps even in the middle of the river junction, where the two branches join to form the Ranu Moi. A massive gold vein has been identified just upstream on the right branch, what is called the Bright River on the map. The mother lode is further inland." I pointed out the place on the map so they were all following me. Of course, they all knew it well.

"You probably remember lots of ground and air survey activity at times during those years." My friends all nodded. That's when they first started the Mambusu Guest Haus to cater for the accommodation demand by surveyors and others engaged in the exploration process. It was a profitable business back then.

"The surveys showed rich deposits of gold and other minerals but no company has proposed to do anything about them yet because of the accessibility problems. It's been considered just too hard to reach the place. The proposal by Namel Mining is expensive and involves huge infrastructure challenges, but they feel it's worth it."

I paused.

"The village of Mambusu will become a town. It will effectively be owned by the company, just like Tabubil town is owned by Ok Tedi, which tightly controls just about every aspect of it. The company will build the infrastructure and train people for their work. The small airstrip will be remade into one capable of bringing in larger passenger and freight aircraft such as Hercules and Dash 8s, and maybe even jets in future. In a few months the Mambusu of today will be unrecognizable. The cost will be your land and your way of life, the benefit will be that Mambusu will become part of the modern world."

I'd always tried to be fair when presenting these proposals to communities. Stating both the positives and negatives seemed to be the honest approach, and generally I felt community leaders appreciated that. I wasn't there to sell the mine concept. I was there to make sure communities understood what they should expect so they could be well informed when it came time for meetings and negotiations between stakeholders.

"The Proposal states that mining is expected to last for seventeen years, with a possibility of another ten years for secondary extraction after that. It'll take five years of building infrastructure before any mining commences. You'll be creating a new world for your children and their children, not yourselves. With that world will come the influx of people from other areas, and a range of social challenges. On the other hand, your children will have opportunities for education and employment, plus the financial benefit of royalties from the company's profits."

I went on to discuss in more detail some of the plans displayed before us. How the mine would need to address the problem of river flow to ensure flood levels, an almost daily occurrence, did not disrupt machinery and flood work sites; how innovative infrastructure such as a train line or a huge tunnel beside the river may be built to transport ore and tailings downstream even as far as the coast itself; how the township would need to have a steady supply of market vegetables and meat to feed the workers, providing opportunities for the local area farmers; and how the building of schools and supermarkets would bring the rest of the world to Mambusu.

We spent several more hours together as they asked question after question. While much of this was informational in nature, helping them understand the technical details of the proposal, I could see they were starting to struggle with the decision they would have to make soon. Is this best for their community or not? How do they decide a future they will not live in? How do they protect their children's future and heritage when their decisions may make it impossible for them to do that?

I began to empathise more and more with my friends and the ethical dilemma they faced. I wished there was some way I could help them more.

I was still struggling with the question as to why I'd felt so drawn to Mambusu all those years ago. Coming back again had felt like coming home in some ways, but the place was different. Yet the way I'd warmed to Lily and my new friends here was different to people in other places I'd visited, even if my government agenda was the same.

Reading grandfather's diary was helping me understand, especially now that I knew he'd actually been at this very location, Mambusu. There were historical family links to this place now. How providential was it that I was reading the diary while being here in the same place, reliving his journey hand in hand with my own. Yet even that didn't explain the link that I felt in my heart with this place.

A fuller explanation of that would come, but it would nearly cost me my life. I decided that I needed to go down to the junction in the river the next day to see both the proposed mine site and where grandfather had camped.

They were, in fact, the same place.

Chapter 15

The Call

I was having breakfast next morning when the call came. The ever-present Lily motioned me over to the phone.

"Justin, it's Kila here," came the voice I recognised immediately as my boss.

"Hi Kila," I replied, a little surprised. "How's things in Moresby?"

"Yeah, busy as normal. Actually, very busy. I need you to come back in to Moresby immediately – something urgent has come up and I need your expertise on it," replied Kila.

"I've only been here a few days, Kila, and our agreement was that I could spend a month here," I retorted. "I'm just starting to make progress with my community liaison here so it's not possible for me to come immediately."

"Yeah, I know I agreed to that. But the Minister is putting pressure on me and I need you here again for a while."

"What is it then that I need to come in for," I asked.

"Oh, it's complicated, in fact too complicated to explain over the phone. But I'll give you a full briefing when you get in. You'll need a few weeks on it by the look of things." Kila didn't sound as convinced or assured about this as he normally was. He always knew exactly what was happening and could clearly explain it. It didn't seem to fit with the Kila I knew so well, but I couldn't argue with him. So I thought I'd try and buy a little more time.

"Ok then… give me three days here and then I'll come, that should enable me to complete the basic level communication I need to do here," I tried to bargain. But he would have none of it.

"Justin, I need you in here today," Kila shot back. "I've ordered a charter flight for you for this morning and that will get you back into Moresby by lunch time."

I had a quick look out the window as Kila spoke, surprised that he was being so directive about getting me out of Mambusu. All I could see was the shroud of mist that so often enveloped the village in the morning. However, this time it was also raining. The sure sign of a bad weather day, and conditions I had no desire to fly in.

"It's a really bad day here Kila," I shot back at him, "and there's Buckley's chance of a *balus* getting in here this morning, so maybe midday in Moresby is a bit ambitious!"

"I'll let the pilot figure that out, just be ready when the plane comes."

End of conversation. Kila sounded under pressure, and that was definitely not the Kila I knew. I'd have to find out why when I got to Moresby.

I was confident it would be several hours before any airplane could find its way up the valley and land at the small Mambusu airstrip. It had been built years earlier when surveys were being conducted to enable easy transportation of company workers in and out of Mambusu. The terrain made it difficult to find a level area and the airstrip site finally chosen was up the side of the mountain behind the village. With a good road now to the area, the airstrip was infrequently used.

Construction of the airstrip had been largely by hand though two tractors with scoops had been brought in once the project started. Villagers from the extended area had been hired to wield shovels and wheelbarrows to chip away the mountainside and fill in the depressions to finally make a smooth runway surface. At 560 metres in length, and a slope of 6.4%, the one-way strip was really only suitable for light aircraft such as single engine Cessna's and Britten Norman Islanders.

The air charter company that usually serviced Mambusu preferred to use its well-worn Cessna 206. The surface condition of the strip easily became soft and boggy from regular rain, and the Islander's dual main wheels only cut deep channels into the soft grass undersurface.

So confident was I that no aircraft would be able to get in to land because of the rain and mist, that I decided to go down to the river junction anyway.

David, John, Lily and I set off down the pathway that led away from the village and down to the Moi River. The track would take us just downstream from the fork, and then follow the river back up to the junction.

The walk down to the Moi River took about 30 minutes, with some slipping and sliding in the wet conditions. We spent another hour walking up to the junction of the rivers and then back into the area in the fork between them. A walking bridge had been constructed some years ago across to the area between the rivers. Consisting of steel cables firmly secured on either side of the river, it was single file only with timber slats wired onto the cables. Up to a quarter of the slats were missing, rotted out or used as firewood, who knows? A second tier of cables at waist height provided a handhold though the bridge would still swing from side to side when anyone walked across it. While the locals took it all in their stride and crossed effortlessly, I felt like my future was definitely in danger and hung on to the cables for dear life.

The area was reasonably flat. While it had obviously been a place of activity in the past, perhaps even a small village site, it was now well grassed over with many small and medium sized trees. Unfortunately I found no direct evidence of grandfather's camp there. I could imagine a gold processing plant here though, and unfolded the development plans I had brought with me, carefully wrapped in plastic, so that my friends could see what was being projected.

It was still drizzling with rain at two o'clock when we arrived back at the Mambusu Guest Haus, boots swimming in slime and legs coated with mud. While the visit to the river junction had been worthwhile, it hadn't given me any unexpected information. To continue across the second river, Bright River, and then up to the site of the gold reef would take a whole day and so would have to wait until I had more time.

As soon as we'd cleaned up, I sat down and sketched a rough map of the area, not to scale, but as best I could visualize it. This helped me appreciate grandfather's movements better as well.

At about 3pm I heard a faint drone, and walked outside to hear the approaching Cessna 206. The weather was still very cloudy though the rain has eased. As it came into view, the aircraft was low. The pilot completed a very low pass over the airstrip as he flew across it to join close downwind and base legs, and then land. He barely had time to straighten his wings on final approach before touching down. The aircraft splashed down and skidded up the runway spraying water like a speedboat. Fortunately the slope provided enough gravitational drag to slow the aircraft down to a walking pace before the pilot slid it deftly into the small parking bay at the top of the airstrip.

"Oh mate!" the nervous young Australian pilot greeted me as he literally jumped out the aircraft, "am I glad to get on the ground!"

I had no reason not to believe him.

"I didn't think I'd make it with all this cloud." He looked nervous and shaken, not a good sign of confidence for an apprehensive passenger like me!

I'd brought my bag with me in anticipation of heading back to Port Moresby with him, but as soon as he saw it he gave me the bad news. "No way am I going back today, mate. This weather is just too bloody bad! I had enough trouble just trying to get here. Is there somewhere I can stay tonight?" My respect for the young pilot, who introduced himself as Mitch, was growing by the minute. Wasn't I right about the weather?

"Yeah, there's a guest house here, where I've been staying actually. It's comfortable and you'll get a good feed tonight."

Glad to hear that he wouldn't have to sleep in the aircraft without a meal, Mitch proceeded to tidy it up for the night, placing some rocks as chocks in front of the wheels. No sooner were we in the front door of the guest haus than it started to rain again.

I was glad for two reasons. Firstly, I wouldn't have to fly out with the weather so bad. Secondly, I'd have time to continue reading grandfather's diary.

Chapter 16

The Elders

Grandfather wrote in detail about deciding to remain in this immediate area and look for the gold vein that was apparently just upriver from the junction.

"I find the local people, who refer to themselves as the Moiaimba, to be very friendly and unconcerned about my presence. The fact that I am looking for their gold doesn't seem to present any anguish and I have come to the conclusion that, because of its accessibility and abundance, it is not seen as valuable in the same sense that we regard it.

"I am not sure about what, if any, use gold is within their culture. I have not to date observed it used in any of their traditional clothing, and because they use no metallic jewelry as such, it seems to have no value. It could be used in trading? What is intriguing is that what the rest of the world considers to be the most precious of minerals is valueless to them! I envy them!

"Perhaps my being here and seeking their gold may start to make them aware that it has value, but I pity the day when they find themselves caught up in exploitation by unscrupulous prospectors who will take advantage of their naivety.

"I have set up a small camp in the fork of the rivers that I will use as a base to explore further towards the upstream site of the gold source according to the Moiaimba description of it. The weather pattern seems to favour a couple of nights

of heavy downpour followed by about two nights of no rain or just passing showers.

"My shelter is made of rough-cut local timber poles about 1" diameter to make a basic frame tied together with vines. Over this the native men I have engaged to help me have attached woven matting made of a bamboo like reed that has been crushed flat. It is very strong and forms a good wall that seems to also keep out larger insects and vermin quite well. On the roof the men have laid bundles of long grass they call kunai to make a very effective and reasonably waterproof roof. I have draped over this a canvas sheet to make sure it is fully waterproof. The doorway is another canvas sheet hung at the top."

. . . .

"Today, a week after my arrival, I was able to visit the village that I was aware of nearby. While I could have forced my presence there earlier, I had decided to wait until I felt there was willingness by the men to offer me some sort of invitation.

"Having some of the village men assisting me with the house building this week has been a good bridge builder with them. They are a jovial lot, full of good humour, and prone to play practical jokes with each other. They have been very willing to teach me their language along the way and so I find myself after one week with a basic grasp of their greetings, some pronouns and some basic nouns and verbs. However their verb conjugations appear complex, and the use of pronouns and subject-object order is difficult to fathom. It seems to relate to who the speaker is, who is being spoken about and the relationship between them. One thing I am fairly clear about is that they refer to each other not by name but by their kinship relationship. They have started calling me "Adi" which I think is a form of brother or uncle, though not their common use of this word. As I get to know the language better, I wonder if it is a term for an outsider whom they accept? That would be nice.

"The village they call Mambusu is about two hours walk away by a track through the jungle. The first obstacle was

to cross the river, only possible when the water level has dropped after rains. With no rain overnight last night, my friends guided me across a section of the river that was wider than normal but also shallower. We waded through in chest deep water with our possessions held above our heads.

"As we reached the top of the hill and entered Mambusu, I was greeted by most of the village inhabitants, assembled ready to see firsthand this foreign visitor to their area. For many it seemed they had not seen a European person before. There was obviously some apprehension, especially by the women and children, who hung back while some of the men came forward to greet me. There was a murmur among the people when I called out a greeting in their language, and I felt their apprehension subside a little.

"With some practice with the builders, and lots of laughter at my attempts, I had learned how to click fingers just as they do to complete a handshake. The apprehension subsided a little more as I shook hands with the elders and impressed them with suitable finger clicks. The smiles of acceptance were clear, and I felt that I also could relax among these newfound friends.

"I have become aware of a principle when engaging with people from another culture that I will try to continue to employ while here. If I try to do things their way, I gain acceptance. If I try to do things my way, I remain aloof and they do not accept me.

"The elders led us to a clearing where we could sit down in a circle, cross-legged on mats on the ground. Fresh coconuts were brought out, gouged out at the top from which to drink like a chalice. The juice was delicious, refreshing and nutritious. It left no doubt in my mind that there was a friendly spirit at work here.

"As only a few of the men speak Motu, and my Moi language is in infancy, our conversation jumped between Motu and Moi, translated to the elders by several of the men.

"Once again I was asked why I was here. I explained that I had come to find the source of the gold that I had seen

at the mouth of their river. This gold was considered valuable to outsiders and used in their jewelry – personal body decorations for special events or ceremonies. I explained that once I had found the gold source, I wished to obtain some of the gold to take back for my family and to sell. I felt that to use my understanding of ceremonial costume and trade in New Guinea to explain my ambitions would be likely to be understood. So I also explained that I wished to find appropriate ways to trade for their gold. As an outsider I had skills and knowledge that I may be able to use to benefit the Moiaimba people in return for the gold.

"I recognise that any venture into the remote parts of New Guinea needs to be conducted cautiously. Forming good relationships with the local people is vital to the success of any prospecting mission. At the same time, it has become clear to me that if I cannot explain my presence in terms that are familiar to the people, I will not be able to gain their trust and acceptance. So it seemed to me that to set the basis of my presence in terms of a trading relationship would be understandable and hopefully acceptable. To me this is exactly what it is, trading gold for what I have of value that I can give to this community.

"The group of village men took some time, perhaps an hour or more, to discuss among themselves, probably grateful that I could not understand them. I began to notice those who were more vocal and those who were more inclined to offer counter advice, perhaps the wisdom of years and experience. At the same time, I recognised the impact that I as an intruder into their community would make. They needed to decide if they felt this was going to be of advantage to them or not.

"Finally the conversation began to drift back to me, and the translation into Motu resumed.

"The elders at first reacted to my audacity in travelling up their river into their terrain without invitation. For my part I had never even considered that common courtesy in gaining an invitation was needed. They recognised that this also took some courage on my part and they respected this. They had heard stories about the changing world and knew that

they would be forced to become part of it in time. So, on one hand they welcomed the opportunity that I would have to help expose them to this wider world.

"On the other hand, they were very wary of outsiders who might corrupt their people and introduce ways that were not in accordance with their cultural traditions. They had been carefully observing me during the past week as they decided if they should allow me to stay or force me to leave.

"I am pleased to report that they felt that what they saw of me was pleasing to them. My willingness to work alongside them building the house and my quick learning of their language and willingness to learn their ways had struck a chord of acceptance with them. They would allow me to stay.

"I expressed my gratitude to them. I would look forward to learning more of their ways and asked them to advise me on how they felt I could assist them. In my own mind was perhaps the opportunity to teach some English or mathematics or grammar, but I felt it important that they identify what they felt I could offer them. In the meantime, they would provide some young men who would work with me to get to the gold source. I was aware that these men would also be watching me closely."

Having established such a positive start to his campaign, grandfather continued to journal his experiences as he moved further upriver, and was able to find the immediate location of the gold vein. His good relationship with the community continued, and it's obvious that he began to develop deep friendships with some of the men. At the same time his visits to the village provided opportunity to treat some of the sick and offer a very basic first aid service. He established his presence in the village now two days a week, and began to sleep overnight in a village house made especially for him. At times, if there was need, this would extend to two or three nights a week, always accompanied by the provision of an evening meal. He would spend his time talking with the elders, learning more about the Moiaimba and their language and customs, and teaching a group of children a little English language and numeracy.

Grandfather's gold prospecting was by all accounts very successful, and while he mentioned little of this in his diary, his three to four days a week spent at the site nearly always yielded some gold. I guess he was reluctant to say too much in his diary in case it fell into the wrong hands.

"It is now six months since I arrived in Mambusu, and while I had expected to have need to return to Port Moresby for supplies and refreshment, and to sell the gold I have accumulated, I find that my integration into village life and ways here is much more fulfilling. The diet of food provided by the villagers, supplemented by my own rations, and the friendship I have with the villagers, is providing all of my needs.

"One of the young single men who has been a constant companion, named Seri, has become like a brother. He is probably about ten years younger than me, but he has welcomed me into his extended family and taught me so much about Moi ways. I am very grateful to him. For several weeks now I have stayed at his family's house in the village rather than the single room house built for me on the outskirts. This has been a wonderful experience and has taught me so much about village life.

"Seri's father is a wonderful gracious man, with wisdom well ahead of his years. He is also part of the clan of leaders in the village. Leadership is passed through the mother to the eldest son. If there is no son, then it is passed to the first grandson, the first son of the daughter.

"I have found myself delighted with Seri's older sister, whose name is Leelak. While the single women in the village are not very visible and kept fairly well out of sight doing menial chores, staying at Seri's family's house has enabled me to meet Leelak. She is the one who does much of the work preparing meals and is a wonderful cook. She has

sparkling eyes and a beautiful smile, and I find myself quite drawn to her vivacious personality.

"I have tried to find out more about cultural practices regarding marriage. It appears the parents and elders choose who will marry, and when the appointed day comes, there is a great celebration. The couple is not permitted to see each other before this event. So it is important that the woman is kept out of sight as much as possible. It appears to be a relationship that brings the clans of the groom and bride together.

"I have come to a point in time where I would like to marry Leelak. It may seem strange for a person such as myself to want to marry a simple village girl in a remote village, but I have found in her everything that I could wish of a wife. I have decided to approach the village head men and discuss this with them".

This was a surprising new twist to grandfather's story, one I had never heard about. A week later, grandfather continued this diary theme again:

"I was able to speak with some of the elders today, including Leelak's father. I was surprised that it was no surprise to them. They said they had been watching me and were aware of the interest I had in Leelak.

"The concept of an outsider marrying one of their women was new, though they suspected it would happen in time. Some of their own men had brought back wives from other tribes after trading trips.

"But their next comments really came as a shock. They had also observed Leelak's feelings towards me, and concluded that she and I would be a good match. They gave their approval, though much more discussion about the traditional payment of dowry was needed. They also stipulated that until the wedding ceremony and feast, I was not to stay at Seri's family house or try to see Leelak. The wedding could be arranged for three months' time as Leelak was already a mature woman and well past marriageable age.

"My heart was merry as I moved back to my single roomed house."

Chapter 17

The Flight

It rained all night, heavy rain that bucketed down. But the fine morning mist gave a clue that it would be a good day once it cleared. I told the pilot not to rush, the fog would take time to clear, and we enjoyed a good breakfast. My heart was happy as I recalled grandfather's news of his marriage. I decided not to take the diary with me to Port Moresby.

By 8 am we were at the aircraft and Mitch conducted his pre-flight checks. Everything appeared normal at first. But when Mitch checked the under-wing fuel drains, the amount of water that drained from them was not. The aircraft had been parked left wing low due to the slope on the parking bay. This meant that it was more difficult to drain out any water that may have made its way into the left wing tank.

"Rats," exclaimed Mitch when he realized the problem, "I can't get all the water out of the downhill tank."

"Is that a problem?" I asked, secretly hoping it would mean another delay of the flight.

"Shouldn't be a problem, I just need to turn the airplane around." While it meant there would be no delay, I was also glad that it wasn't an airplane problem. So our flight would proceed after all.

The fuel caps, found on the top of the wings on the Cessna 206, are known to sometimes let water in during overnight rain. This is especially the case with aircraft that have not had the rubber O-ring around the cap changed or lubricated for some time. Fortunately Mitch was basically aware of this, and gave me a quick lesson on fuel caps as he worked. He wisely asked me to assist him turn the aircraft around in the parking bay so that he could check for water contamination with the left wing high. This meant that any water in the tank would flow towards the wing root where the drain plug was.

The right wing drain had produced nearly 300 ml of water, enough to be of concern. Mitch kept draining it out from the under-wing drain plug until there was only AVGAS draining. With the left wing now high, he again drained nearly 250 ml of water from that wing tank.

Satisfied that we had nothing but aviation fuel left in the tanks now, Mitch called me on board and made sure I was strapped in. Rather than sit beside him in the right hand co-pilot seat, he asked me to sit behind him on the left. This would help counter the right wing heavy tendency he would experience because there was much more fuel in the right tank. I obliged, though would have had a better view of the valley from the front seat.

"Moresby, this is Airtaxi 14, taxying at Mambusu for Port Moresby, two persons on board." I heard Mitch give his taxying call as he completed the engine run up and magneto checks, and moved out onto the airstrip to take off. It was a beautiful sight, perched at the top of the strip looking down into the valley. The fog had almost cleared and the mountains and valleys in front of us were perfectly clear and majestic. They more than matched grandfather's wonderful descriptions. I was glad we'd waited overnight as this would be a great flight in to Port Moresby, and I was glad to be able to get a perfect aerial view of the rivers and junction as we flew past.

Holding the brakes on, Mitch ran the engine up to full power and then, releasing the brakes, allowed the aircraft to accelerate with a jerk. We were airborne two thirds of the way down the airstrip. What a glorious day it was as I started to scan down the river looking for clues from grandfather's account of his journey here.

We'd climbed no more than 500 feet when the engine surged and quit.

Silence.

All I could hear was the hiss of wind rushing against the airplane.

Mitch was frantic, pushing buttons and pulling levers, wanting desperately to restart the engine, but having no success. I could see that he was trying to go through emergency drills. In the eerie silence of those seconds, I heard him talk his way through setting up for a glide and switching fuel tanks. But there was no response from the engine.

Mitch was left with a dilemma now. He couldn't turn back to Mambusu airstrip, it was now too far away. There was no other option left but to land in the trees that lined the mountain sides or try for the flatter aspect of the land in the junction of the rivers. Any landing must be uphill rather than downhill to enable the aircraft to land at the lowest speed possible. So, as we glided down the valley I realised that Mitch was now commencing a turn back up towards the fork in the rivers. It crossed my mind that the mine site was now going to be the crash site.

It's apparently amazing what goes through a person's mind when faced with the prospect of death. I'd read all sorts of stories from people who faced death and were spared. Scenes from their life flashed past them, and a panic from not knowing what the next minutes will reveal seized them.

I didn't experience any of that, just a quiet assurance that this was not the end. I believe that God had put me on earth for a purpose and that purpose had not been fulfilled, so I wouldn't die, yet! I also hoped this wasn't just wishful thinking!

I had no idea what was going on in Mitch's mind. I could only see him from behind, setting the aircraft up for a landing into the trees upriver from the fork. He did well, but could do nothing to avoid the inevitable. In the last final seconds of the flight he masterfully guided the aircraft into a controlled stall into the trees. It was obvious that he'd selected an area with lighter trees, and I wanted to commend him for his airmanship.

The noise as we crashed through the tree canopy was deafening. The silence of the last two minutes was suddenly interrupted as metal and wood collided, plastic smashed and branches scratched paint. I'd braced myself by putting my head forward almost between my knees while folding my hands over my head. The final impact was much gentler than I'd expected as tree branches began to absorb the momentum of the aircraft, which had already lost its left wing, wheels and most of the tail section. I could smell fuel.

With a final lurch, the aircraft came to rest amongst foliage with its nose and wingless left side down. We were suspended about a metre above the ground. By now I was holding my head in my hands and had only one thought as the noise once again dwindled to nothing. 'Get out of the aircraft before it catches fire!'

Mitch didn't move. I could only see that his head had smashed against the instrument panel. I'd get myself out first and then drag him out. As I started to free myself from the seat belt and smash the pilot's window to get out of the airplane though, I discovered my right foot was jammed. The pilot's seat had moved back during the final impact and my foot was now crushed under it. Sudden panic rushed over me, fueled by the increasingly strong smell of AVGAS - highly flammable aviation petrol.

It was now obvious that my ankle had been broken. So far there was no pain, but it would come. I managed to manoeuvre my foot out from under the pilot's seat and then the pain hit. There was no blood visible so it appeared that it was an internal fracture, though my foot must have been quite bruised. Reaching forward I pulled the handle on the pilot's door and was able to force it open enough to give me an exit. Letting myself down through branches on my good leg and hands, I made it to the ground. I needed to consider a rescue plan for Mitch before getting as far away from the aircraft as I could in case it caught fire and exploded. But as I looked back into the aircraft, I could see quite clearly that any rescue was already too late. I was the only survivor.

I wasn't sure exactly where we'd landed except that it was further upriver from the junction of the two rivers. I had no doubt that help would be on the way soon. Little did I know that Mitch hadn't been able to get through on his initial radio call, and so aviation authorities had no knowledge that he'd even taken off. Fortunately people in the local Mambusu community had heard the engine fail and knew the aircraft had turned upstream to land in the jungle, but it would take nearly a day for villagers to find the site.

My first concern was to get away from the aircraft to safety. So I crawled through the jungle until I felt I was at a safe distance before considering how to find the best place to wait. Experts always say to stay close to the aircraft. Initially I just rested where I was, my aching foot flopping around without the bracing of its bones. I'd need to find some way to bind it up. As time progressed and moved past midday, I began to think about the possibility of spending the night here. So it seemed wise to try and build a makeshift shelter. I reached out to gather some branches and leaves and make a kind of shelter around me. The pain in my foot was excruciating and I tried to keep it still and immobilized.

After an hour or so I'd made myself a rough canopy though doubted it would keep me dry if it rained. Exhausted, and with my aching ankle starting to swell, I collapsed where I lay and began to doze off. The adrenalin rush of the last few hours had given way to exhaustion. My mouth was parched. I was thankful at least there had been no fire, but heartbroken for Mitch. He'd set the aircraft up so well for landing, and inadvertently saved my life by putting me in the middle seat.

I awoke midafternoon, somewhat bewildered. At first I couldn't figure out where I was. The pain in my ankle when I moved my leg reminded me. No help had arrived. I wondered when it would come, even if it would come.

Lying there in the jungle I became aware of some movement to one side. Through a tunnel in the undergrowth I could see a small bird on the ground perhaps ten metres away. It was in a small cleared area and cleaning the ground of twigs and leaves with its beak. With beautiful black plumage and what looked like a blue breastplate and white spot above its beak, I recognised this as one of the rare Birds of Paradise. Usually only seen mummified and adorning ceremonial headdresses, I understood that I was being treated to a special performance, probably a courting ritual.

As I watched, making sure I didn't make any movement, the bird began to dance. Suddenly its plumage changed, like it reversed its feathers, its shape changed, and with iridescent black sparkling feathers displayed like a skirt, it bobbed up and down and stepped from side to side in ritual dance. Its shape reminded me of something familiar but in this state of mind I couldn't recall what.

With several long feathers which looked like sticks with pompoms at the end jutting up from its head, the bird danced around bobbing from side to side, which made the head feathers also wobble from side to side. It was a comical display. But the crowning masterpiece was its breastplate. In the middle of its chest was a mesmerizing dish of feathers that sparkled different colours as the bird bobbed around and flicked this breastplate at different angles. Brilliant reds, yellows, greens, blues and violets danced around its chest in random radiation in the midst of its polished choreography. I couldn't have imagined anything more spectacular in nature than this.

Spellbound I watched, treated to a spectacle few others in the world had ever had the privilege of enjoying. With suitor suitably impressed, the bird leaped into the branches above me to complete the ritual, unfortunately out of my sight. It was all over in minutes but I'd remember every dance step for the rest of my life. How profound that in the midst of the agony and pain of this accident I would find such incredible beauty. My body ached but my heart sang.

As sunset approached I resigned myself to spending the night in the jungle. But the jungle was no longer a place of fear. I'd witnessed the most wonderful of nature's gifts, and was safe here.

Fortunately there was no rain that night. The rainwater that had worked its way into the aircraft's fuel tanks and fuel collector bowl, as the investigation of Mitch's accident subsequently revealed, had vented its fury and found its target. It no longer held any power over me.

Chapter 18

The Visit

Kila Woro picked up the phone, answering its nagging ring. He'd only just received news of the crash a few hours earlier. With no word on Justin or the pilot's fate, he was worried. Justin had been his friend for many years. They'd worked together in the Department of Social Resources and come up through the ranks to where they were now. Justin had been a welcome friend to his family and often visited their home. He was Uncle Justin to his kids. He'd attended their church often, and always been invited to attend special family gatherings. He, Kila, had been responsible for ordering Justin into Port Moresby and felt directly responsible for the accident. If Justin was dead, he would never forgive himself.

"Kila," spoke the Member for Moi, "what's this I hear about a plane crash at Mambusu? What can you tell me?"

"Well I've only just heard about it but it was the aircraft sent in to collect Justin Orlando. I ordered him to leave to get him out of your way. But I have no news of the crash except that Justin was on board." Kila was fighting to keep away the tears, and his voice wavered as he finished his sentence.

"Hey, bro," shot back Lupo Warina, "if he's dead, that's the end of our worries about him. Your plan may have been more successful that you imagined! I should let you know that the meeting with the community I planned for tomorrow at

Mambusu will still go ahead. So if he's still alive I want you to make sure he's not anywhere near there. I hope you understand me. Call me back as soon as you know what happened with the plane."

Without waiting for a reply, Honourable Lupo Warina, Member for Moi, hung up the phone.

Kila slowly put the phone receiver back in its place. He knew that he'd now become a puppet of the Member, and didn't like it. He realized he'd let himself get trapped into an evil scheme from which he couldn't escape. He felt disgusted with himself and ashamed that he'd allowed himself to fall into the Member's grip so easily.

Last night, late in the evening, two large pigs had been delivered to his house. Gifts towards his son's bride price. He knew who'd sent them and how they'd been paid for.

His career was now in the balance, his future blurred as he contemplated being discovered, or serving life as a slave of the Member. He decided that he now had a choice. He'd succumbed to corruption but he wouldn't allow it to consume him.

He would become a double agent. While appearing to serve the Member he would in fact help Justin, even if he was dead, discretely making sure he was always one step ahead of the Member. He'd make sure that the Member didn't succeed in his corrupt plans to exploit the Moiaimba people.

Kila sat down, the rest of his life now a blank slate in his mind, and began to form a strategy. He paused for a quick prayer. "Papa God, I have sinned and done the wrong thing. Please forgive me, in Jesus' name, and help me find a way to do the right thing to expose this evil."

The first essential was to know whether Justin had survived the plane crash. In that case he'd work with him.

But if Justin was dead, then he'd need to find out more about what the Member was up to. The place to start was to find out more about Moi Futures Ltd.

Chapter 19

The Recovery

I can't remember much after witnessing the bird dance. The impact on me must have been to bring a peace I would otherwise not have known. I woke next morning as first light approached hearing the beautiful sounds of Birds of Paradise in the jungle.

The pain in my swollen foot brought me to my senses quickly and I was thankful to be dry still. Longing for a drink of water, I heard the sound of water splashing over rocks in the distance. The river. I'd need to get myself there.

No sign of help yet. I hope it comes soon. I take stock of my bearings and begin to crawl towards the sound of the river. The jungle is thick and my foot aches at every move. After just two metres of crawling, dragging my gammy leg I'm already sweating. My mouth is dry. My body aches all over. It was pushed around in the accident and is now complaining. I rest and try again.

It seemed like hours later but was probably only one when I reached the river's edge, pulled myself onto the stony shoreline, and scooped up a handful of water. Water had never tasted so good. Exhausted, I collapsed again into unconsciousness.

The men were leaning over me, shaking me. Pain shot through my leg and foot as they tried to lift me. With a shout, as much as I could muster in my weakened state anyway, I pointed at my foot. They could see for themselves the odd angle that it now held against my leg. I recognised some of their faces.

Then a woman's voice called through the cacophony of sounds I was hearing - water splashing, men talking among themselves, the rattle of people running over river rocks, and people shouting in the distance. It was the most beautiful voice I'd ever heard, and I knew to whom it belonged.

"Justin," she called as she came slipping over rocks to reach me, "are you alright?"

I raised my eyes to see Lily bending down to cradle my head. I gave her a half nod but she knew as well as I did that I was lying.

"Oh, it's so good to see you are alive, I was sure you must have died in the *balus*. The boys are making a bush stretcher to carry you back to Mambusu."

I knew I was in safe hands now, but having Lily with me gave me added strength and comfort. She would take care of me.

I had no idea what time it was but the men wasted no time strapping me to a couple of raw timber poles laced with vines that made a stretcher. Soon I was lifted up and we began the long walk home. I learned later that the men had camped just downriver the night before, as far as they could get before darkness set in. They knew they wouldn't find us in the dark so had set out at first light following the river, and found me soon afterwards. Others had then discovered the aircraft nearby, and Mitch's fate, and that was what they were shouting about in the distance when I first heard Lily. It was probably no later than about 8am.

I drifted in and out of consciousness and remember very little of my ride back to Mambusu. On the few occasions I opened my eyes I could see Lily walking beside the stretcher. She was vocal in her directions to the men and her voice became my reassurance during the journey.

We arrived back at Mambusu just before sunset. I realize now that the men had walked fast to cover the distance while carrying the stretcher, often through narrow jungle paths or over river rocks. I have no idea how they manhandled me over the steel cable bridge. But there was now a bond of gratefulness, a debt of gratitude, that existed between myself and this community. It was something that I could not repay but would be obligated to for life.

Lily had set up a room in the guest haus as a triage centre in preparation for any survivors. When people in the community raised word of the aircraft crash, authorities in Port Moresby had been contacted. A response team had been dispatched immediately by helicopter, and this included a medical team with a doctor. While my broken ankle and bruised foot was in poor condition, I had lost no blood. I was given painkillers and put to sleep while the medical team set my ankle and bandaged it tight in preparation for the flight to Port Moresby, this time by helicopter.

When I woke from the sedative induced sleep an hour later I was informed that it'd been decided to remain in Mambusu overnight, for two reasons. First of all, it was too late for the helicopter because it couldn't fly at night. Secondly, my general condition was considered too poor and so the opportunity to rest overnight would give me a chance to start my recovery. My injuries were not at all life threatening, but the combination of broken leg, surviving the accident and a night in the bush had knocked me around and left me dehydrated.

Once the effects of the anaesthetic had worn off, Lily arranged my transfer back to my own room. I noticed the chair beside my bed.

"I'm staying with you, Justin," she said as they lifted me back onto my bed, "to look out for you during the night."

Of course, I had absolutely no objections at all!

Lily had arranged some food and a cup of tea for me. As we sat in silence while I ate, I began to reflect again on grandfather's diary, and the revelations of his upcoming marriage. The painkillers were working now and my mind was able to focus again.

"Lily, can I ask you a question?" I asked.

"Yes, certainly, what is it you want to know?" she replied without giving any hint of feeling vulnerable.

"Where did you get your name?"

The little I knew about Moiaimba culture and names had led me to believe that Lily was not a traditional name.

"Oh, I was given this name in memory of my grandfather's sister. Her name was Leelak, but my parents called me Lily."

A sudden sense of excitement grabbed me and I'm sure my heart began racing at double speed!

"Do you know much about her, Lily?" I ventured to explore this lineage with her.

"Well, they say she was a beautiful woman, very intelligent and very kind. She died quite young unfortunately, so that's why my family wanted to remember her through me. I feel it's an honour to be named after her." I could sense the pride Lily felt.

"Oh, I'm sorry to hear that. Do you know how she died?" I asked. I needed to know more about Leelak. Here I was with her direct descendant, Lily, named after her. How much closer to grandfather could I get?

Whether Lily was unwilling to disclose something to me that was so personal to her, or whether she genuinely had other business, I will never know. But she politely ended the conversation and excused herself.

"Now that you are awake again, I'll have to leave you for a little while. I need to go and attend to some urgent Guest Haus business." With that Lily walked purposefully out of my room, closing the door quietly behind her.

Chapter 20

The Operation

Dosed up on painkillers, I must have slept well. When I awoke next morning, Lily was beside me again. Dreams of the little bird dancing were fresh on my mind. I decided not to tell anyone about it yet.

But I did start to consider how lucky I was to have been treated to this display that still stirred my heart. As hard as it was, I decided that I wouldn't even tell Lily about it, or reveal anything to her about my grandfather marrying Leelak, until I was ready.

The doctor told me that I couldn't eat because I'd be taken straight into surgery in Port Moresby Private Hospital on arrival. After some breakfast, which everyone except me enjoyed, a stretcher was prepared to carry me to the helicopter that was parked in the school grounds. I was thankful that I wouldn't need to be carried the kilometre uphill to the airstrip. My leg hurt but I was given more painkillers for the trip.

A phone call came in to the Guest Haus, intercepted by Lily. After she'd hung up the phone, she relayed the message to me.

"That was your boss, Kila," she said. "He said he was very glad that you survived the accident and would see you in Port Moresby when you get in. He wanted you to know that the Member was planning to visit Mambusu later today. He said he was sorry you couldn't be there after all, but perhaps you could delegate someone to attend the meetings on our behalf."

My mind wasn't fully switched on to what was going on around me and so I didn't pick up the nuances of Kila's comments. But I did register that I should ensure there was representation at the Member's community meetings. As I was being carried out to the helicopter, a number of community leaders stepped up to wish me well. I managed to let Council President John Aitomo know what Kila had said. He assured me that there would definitely be ears and eyes at the Member for Moi's meetings this time.

Kila was at the Port Moresby airport to meet us as he expected, and had arranged an ambulance to take me to the private hospital. There'd been a spare seat in the helicopter, so Lily came with me. Kila had obviously had some contact with the doctors as well. It's standard practice in Port Moresby to have to buy one's own medical supplies before going into surgery, and Kila had everything well prepared. I'd be forever grateful for his assistance.

The next 24 hours are a blur. I woke from surgery with a plaster cast over my lower leg. The surgery had been successful and a metal plate had been screwed in to join the broken bones. However I'd be bedridden for one to two weeks and then on crutches for several weeks. Once again Kila bent over backwards to attend to me, and nothing seemed too hard for him. I felt very grateful for this brother and his family who brought me food and cared for me. Of course, that care extended to Lily as well, who still never left my bedside and introduced me to her brothers and sister who came to visit me.

On the second day after my operation I was cleared to leave the hospital. I said to Kila that I'd actually prefer to go back to Mambusu to recuperate, knowing that I'd be well looked after by Lily and the community. To my surprise Kila was enthusiastic about it.

"I think that's a great idea, Justin. I've already put in your application and approved six weeks medical leave. The best place for you is back in Mambusu. To tell you the truth, I think the Member is up to something and it'll be good to have you on the spot there. Did I tell you that he had some mining company representatives with him when he visited Mambusu the day you were flown out? Anyway, I've arranged a helicopter to take you back whenever you want."

Lily accompanied me back to my unit in Korobosea to help me pack a few extra things on the way to the airport. I'd already decided that I'd take grandfather's rosewood chair back to Mambusu. I missed it and it'd give me a comfortable chair to sit in. I'd need that in the coming weeks.

I wasn't ready for Lily's reaction though when she walked in and saw the chair, in pride of place in my lounge room. She seemed to catch her breath, paused, and slowly walked towards it, just staring at it. I'm sure I saw her face start to go white!

"Lily, are you ok?" I asked, ready to support her if she fainted, but knowing I had no way to do that on only one good leg and crutches.

"The chair," she replied almost in a whisper, "the chair…. where did you get it?" She sat herself down in a lounge chair, still staring at grandfather's chair.

"Do you like it? I want to take it back to Mambusu. Why Lily, why do you ask?" I wasn't prepared to disclose too much just yet but realized this chair must have had some significance for her.

"I've heard of it, I've heard stories about it." She was pensive and a little apprehensive but in the end made the decision to tell me more. "It's like the one that was made by the gold prospector who married my grandfather's sister. My people tell stories about it." Lily was relaxing a little now. "Look at the carvings, they are pictures from my tumbuna lain, cultural stories and traditions."

Lily bent forward to look at the carvings a little closer, reaching out and daring to touch the chair and stroke the carvings. It was awesome to see the way she approached the chair with a reverence, respect and even a love for the connection it gave her with the past.

"Justin, tell me, where did you get it from?" she asked me once more.

But I was now beginning to be engrossed in the chair and its carvings again myself. The upside-down cup shaped carvings so prominent on the front arm supports particularly. Suddenly these strange shapes became recognizable, I now knew what they were. The little bird when it danced. But I wondered why grandfather would have carved that into the chair?

"Lily, tell me about the stories in the carvings, can you?" I kept stalling her until I could find out more myself.

"The chair, its… oh, it is so beautiful, much more beautiful than the stories can describe. The gold prospector made it over many months after he married my grandmother's sister. The stories tell how he went out into the bush to find the best rosewood tree. They say he carved it from one single piece of wood. He would spend hours every day just chiseling away. At first no one knew what he was doing but then they started to see the chair take shape. He listened to our traditional stories and we began to see pictures of those stories in the carvings. The progress of the chair was the constant news in the village."

She paused again to look around at the other side of the chair. "Look, here's the crocodile. We have lots of stories about crocodiles on the coast, stories of traders being taken by them and others escaping from them."

Again she asked, "Justin, please tell me, where did you get the chair from?"

"What about these circular sort of cup shaped carvings on the front legs Lily, what stories do they come from?" I asked, trying to delay answering her one more time.

"I don't know what they are," she said quite sincerely, "but they're probably some story that the gold prospector knew that I don't."

"Does the chair have any significance for the leadership of the clan do you know?" I asked her, pushing my luck with one more question.

"Oh yes, our stories say that the chair was made for the headman, like a throne chair, but that when the gold prospector left he took it with him. He said that the person who came back with the chair in future would be their headman. That story is legendary."

Now it was my turn to be stunned. I caught my breath and sat down in the chair closest to me – which happened to be grandfather's rosewood chair. What had she said? That the person who came back with the chair would be their headman?

Lily interrupted my thoughts. "So I'm not answering any more questions until you tell me what you are doing with this chair, Justin?"

I knew my time was up and I had to tell her the truth.

"There's something I have to tell you Lily." I began and then paused to take a deep breath. "The gold prospector, the man who made this chair and married your grandfather's sister.... he is my grandfather."

Lily stared at me, then stared at the chair, and then back at me. She was lost for words, but finally she said, "You mean…. you mean… this chair is yours?"

I nodded.

"Several years ago my grandfather passed away and he left me this chair in his estate," I said. "I had no idea that the chair had meaning but I started to restore it. He'd told me nothing about any journey to PNG or anything about the chair. In fact, no one in our family knew. Then I found his diary, you know, the one you found on the floor the first night I was in Mambusu. It was hidden in the seat of the chair. It was the record of his gold prospecting days, marrying Leelak and his time in Mambusu".

My eyes were filling with tears and from what I could see, so were Lily's. This revelation was so amazing, so life changing for both of us.

"I can see it now, it all makes sense," she blurted out.

"What makes sense?" I queried with a quivering voice.

"Well, since you came everything has seemed different…. from the moment you walked in the door at the Guest Haus I knew there was something special about you. Not because you're a senior government worker or anything like that, but something in my spirit jumped and I've just felt this amazing bond with you. I couldn't explain it, and couldn't fight it. And when I found you on the riverbank after thinking you'd died in the plane crash, I was just so relieved. It's like you belong here, but more than that, it's like this is your *ples*, your home. Having you here has brought a stability to the people. They trust you. I don't know how else to explain it."

Wow, I didn't expect that! But Lily's revelation was crystal clear – I owned the chair. I was the next headman of the Moiaimba!

Chapter 21

The Agreement

The Member for Moi, Honourable Lupo Warina, had prepared well for his visit to Mambusu. As his helicopter approached Mambusu, he noticed another one that had just taken off, and presumed that it was evacuating Justin Orlando. He was correct. He mentally noted how well Kila had arranged this.

While the people of Mambusu were barely aware of his visit, or so he hoped, he'd made sure that a large contingent from his own village of Deria would come down the hill to Mambusu. As his helicopter, chartered by Namel Mining Pty Ltd, landed he was pleased to see a large group of his people waiting for him.

Accompanying the Member were several Namel Mining senior executives, all from South East Asia. The Member had insisted that they couldn't add any more people to his party on this helicopter trip, and so there were no Papua New Guinean representatives from Namel Mining present. The Member was glad that his plan to ensure that none of the Namel Mining executives would be able to understand the proceedings had worked. The South East Asians seemed to barely speak English and would have no hope listening to the occasional Tok Pisin that might be mixed up in the Moi language he would be using. He would ensure their understanding of the proceedings would be exactly what he wanted them to understand.

What the Member didn't know was that John Aitomo had quickly met with Umbare David, Paul Wondango, the School Principal, and Hendros Kipa, local businessman. They had in turn decided to ensure that as many people as possible from Mambusu shadowed the Member to be sure his every word was heard. In little over an hour they'd also assembled a group that in fact comprised nearly all of the village of Mambusu, though the representatives from Deria may still have slightly outnumbered those from Mambusu. While the Derians came for the party, the Mambusuans came to protect their land. They were by now assembling in the school grounds where the Member would address everyone.

Leading his mining company colleagues from the helipad to the school grounds, the Member looked like he was in his finest moment. Proud and confident, this was his chance to show off not only the proposed site but also his authority and standing in the community. He was going to impress these mining men so that the success of their proposal was absolutely beyond doubt before a drill had even turned.

A small shelter had been built in one corner of the school sports ground. With a frame of small trees cut from just behind the school, and draped in leaves and kunai grass, it enabled the visitors to sit in the shade and be elevated about a metre above the crowd. An amplifier had been found and it joined the dignitaries on the platform to provide ample volume for all to hear their speeches.

Mr Warina made his way majestically through his crowd of supporters, shaking hands furiously as he led his party to the platform. His representative took the microphone and turned around to make sure all the dignitaries were seated before turning back to face the crowd.

"Ol manmeri bilong Mambusu," he began, "Ladies and Gentlemen of Mambusu, I wish to welcome the Member for Moi, Honourable Lupo Warina…" he paused to ensure the crowd clapped their hands, and gestured to make sure they did. The irony that the majority of the crowd was in fact from Deria was not lost on the Member.

His representative continued "… and senior delegates from Namel Mining Pty Ltd. The future of the Moiaimba is in good hands – the hands of our Member. Already he has achieved so much for our area. Recognising the potential that gold exploration has for our region, our Member has taken extraordinary initiative to make sure that any future development of our gold resources fully benefits the people of his electorate.

"Ladies and Gentlemen, today our Member has invited senior officials from Namel Mining to personally visit Mambusu and see for themselves the area that, under their management, will become Papua New Guinea's largest gold mine. This mine will bring unparalleled benefits to the Moiaimba people. I ask you to enthusiastically welcome these three gentlemen from South East Asia to Mambusu."

He paused and once again gestured to make sure the crowd clapped their hands enthusiastically.

"And now, I welcome to the microphone our Member, Honourable Lupo Warina." Stepping back, he handed the microphone to the Member.

"Ladies and Gentlemen ….." Lupo paused to allow the clapping to subside, "… thank you for your very warm welcome today." The Member had now slipped into Moi language, assuring all that he was truly one of them.

He continued, "Today is an honourable occasion. To have these three senior executives from Namel Mining visit Mambusu has marked this day indelibly on our calendar. In the years ahead we will look back on this day and say, this is the day we started down a new road, a road to prosperity, development, education and opportunity for our people. This is the day we said to the rest of PNG and the world that we are a progressive people, a people with ambition and desire, a people who have the future of our children as our primary interest, and a people who are not going to let obstacles stop us from finding the best way to make our natural resources work for us."

The Member paused to allow for applause, and was not disappointed.

"Let me be more specific," the Member continued, changing the tone of his voice ever so slightly to ensure he now had that 'you can trust me' edge to it. "Over the last year I have been working closely with Namel Mining and the gentlemen here with me."

The Member knew this was stretching the truth because he had not set eyes on these men until he joined them in the helicopter. But he'd made contact with some of their SE Asian government representatives, and had been in liaison with Namel Mining's PNG managers.

"During that time we have worked together to develop a complex set of plans that will see the fulfillment of our dream. I'm sure many of you have seen those plans and fully concur with the exciting developments they contain.

"I'm here today to announce that within one year, Namel Mining plans to commence Stage One infrastructure development. That development will mean that Mambusu town will become a truly international and world-class community. Not only will there be accommodation and other facilities built to house the mine staff, but a small hospital and high school will be built within the next five years."

A roar of approval went up from the crowd, which launched into clapping and cheering.

"Within seven years the mine will be in full operation. Mambusu will be known around the world, and its sealed highway and airport upgraded to take commercial airliners such as Dash 8s will have opened the world to us."

Again, cheering and clapping.

"But there is more. The part that I am most proud of, and pleased to announce today, is that I have negotiated with Namel Mining for the Moiaimba people to receive a 15% share of profits from the mine. These will be administered through a special trust that I have set up, called the Namel Community Trust fund. This fund is fully accountable under Namel Mining, and the 15% community dividend will be included in the agreement between Namel Mining and the Government of PNG. This means that your share of the profits is absolutely 100% safe."

In a climate where many thought the only safe money was that already in the politician's pocket, many people were rightly suspicious. But at this news, a huge cheer rose from the crowd. The Member was convincing in his rhetoric, and there was no doubt that he had enticed many people into a new level of trust in his schemes.

He continued his speech for a few more minutes but his main impact had been achieved. The Namel Mining representatives could see the community support he had. This speech was well prepared and the executives had been given copies of it word for word in their own language. Everything was transparent here, there could be no doubt about the Member's authority in his community.

On their departure the executives would be treated to a low helicopter fly past of the river junction and a fly along the river in which the gold flowed. But before having a lunch that had been hastily arranged at the Mambusu Guest Haus, the Member and his guests sought a meeting with selected Moiambamatuan people of influence. It was at this meeting that David, John, Paul and Hendros must be present. Quickly they discussed their strategy to infiltrate it. Even if Lily had been there she wouldn't have attended, to keep a low profile. It was a pity however that she wouldn't be able to be at the lunch - her ability to listen in on conversations at the Guest Haus was legendary! Who would have suspected that the waitress was actually the lawyer who may spearhead any counter challenge to the mine?

Paul Wondango, the Head Teacher at the school, had been invited to the meeting – it was to be held in one room at his school after all. Umbare David, because of his senior position in the community, was also invited, as was John Aitomo. At the front door a minimal security presence had been established with two ambivalent, hastily arranged guards. John was able to convince them that Hendros should also have been invited, and they all were let in. Once inside the room, it became very apparent that the fifty, perhaps sixty others in the room were far more representative of Deria than Mambusu.

The Member's representative once again introduced the meeting using a microphone and the same amplifier. A table had been prepared, complete with white paper tablecloth, and the Member and his visitors sat behind it. On the table David and John noticed a set of plans that were identical to the ones Justin had showed them just days earlier.

"Ladies and Gentlemen, thank you for attending this special meeting. The Member has wished to provide more detail about the mining proposal to you, recognizing you as leaders in this community. I'll hand over to him now."

No applause this time.

The Member took the microphone from his representative and rose to speak.

"Leaders of this community, thank you for attending this special meeting, and please thank your people for their fantastic support shown to us today. There is no doubt that this venture has got off to a magnificent start today.

"The purpose of this meeting is twofold. Firstly, I want to display to you the Proposal plans so that you can see first hand the development planned for Mambusu. I invite you to come and view these plans at the conclusion of this meeting. My representative here will be able to explain them to you if you have any questions."

With this the representative held up one of the A4 bound documents and unfolded one of the colour maps. While it only contained a colourful display of geological survey information, it looked very impressive to many of those gathered.

The exceptions were David, John, Hendros and Paul, who already had an in-depth understanding of the Proposal, thanks to Justin's briefings. They'd been certain to make sure they'd also discussed the plans with a number of other influential Mambusu residents and landowners. So while the Member was sure that he'd impressed many, he had in fact only impressed the Deria contingent who were, so far, ignorant of his plans for this development.

"You'll see that we have already put a lot of time and effort into these plans and they're at final approval stage. That means they are almost ready to commence Stage One. You'll find all the details of Stage One in this folder," and he pointed to one of the books on the desk in front of him. "I've personally been over and over these plans in fine detail and can assure you that everything here has the best interests of our people as its first objective.

"The second reason for this meeting is to arrange for agreement to a mining lease here at Mambusu to start up the project. We've drawn up a survey of the land required on this map of the area," he held up a map, "and now wish to proceed with the lease agreement.

"As you can see, I'm doing all I can to make sure that you, the Moiaimba people, gain maximum benefit from this mine venture. So I'm asking now for representatives from the community to come forward and sign up. Under the Agreement a minimum of forty signatories is required from people who are recognised community leaders and landowners."

There was silence as the group listened to the Member and his quite extraordinary proposal to lease Mambusu to Namel Mining.

John Aitomo raised his voice, "Member, I have a question."

"Yes Council President, we'll have to keep this meeting moving but go ahead with your question," the Member replied.

"Thank you Honourable Member. My question is this. You say that the mining company wishes to operate its mining venture here. The land it wishes to lease is the entire land holdings of Mambusu village and surrounds for approximately three kilometers. You say that Namel Mining will release funds deposited into the Namel Community Trust fund. It seems to me that by doing this you are asking us to relinquish our land long term to a mining company. Can you please advise this meeting exactly what the terms and conditions are, what the value is, and what the relationship between Namel Mining and Namel Community Trust fund is?"

John Aitomo left the Member in no doubt that a direct and specific answer was required. There was no room for political excuses or verbal ducking for cover here. The Member and everyone in the room recognised this.

"Well, thank you for your question, Council President. First of all, I must assure you that all dealings with the mining company will be conducted with total transparency. You have my pledge of assurance on that. So whatever arrangements are in place, I have insisted that they are in the best interests of yourselves, the Moiaimba community." John and his friends noted that the Member referred to the Moiaimba community, not the Mambusu community that was really the community in question.

The Member continued. "The terms and conditions of the land lease will be fully and legally drawn up and approved so that there is no room for ambiguity or doubt. Namel Mining must have absolute ability to conduct their operations on the land, and a comprehensive lease is the best policy. The lessee of the land will actually be the Namel Community Trust on behalf of Namel Mining, so lease benefits will actually flow straight back to you, the landowners.

"While the Namel Community Trust is a subsidiary company of Namel Mining, you can see quite clearly that it is set up as a trust fund for the local community. Full power and control of the funds rests with you, the community, through the Board. Once the mining company has completed operations and withdraws, you will be able to lease back the land through the Namel Community Trust fund at peppercorn rental. The trust fund will actually fund something like 95% of your future lease costs. So the land will effectively remain yours.

"Gentlemen, as you can see, this is an absolute win for the Moiaimba community. You will receive a massive payment for lease of your land, the invested money will be managed through the trust fund which will manage infrastructure development in the community on behalf of the company. And at the end of it you will be able to keep your land for a very minimal lease cost because the majority of lease costs will be met through the trust fund."

The Member paused, looking for signs that his explanation had met with a chord of approval with the crowd. To say that he was disappointed is an understatement. While a few gullible Derian's fell for his explanation, it was clear that the majority had serious questions about it still. These questions were very much about what the real cost of relinquishing their land was.

John spoke up again. "Member, thank you for that explanation. I have one more question because you didn't answer all of my previous questions. What is the relationship between Namel Mining and the Namel Community Trust fund, and who are the Board members of the trust fund? We have not heard of this trust fund before and we need to know who the Directors are."

"Ah yes, President," the Member replied, "the trust fund was my initiative during my discussions with the company. I wished to ensure there was a credible and transparent route for funds such as royalties, dividends and proceeds of land leases to be available for the community. Our legal advice was to establish a trust fund under Namel Mining, which is what I've done. Namel Mining appointed myself as Chairman of the trust fund, knowing that I could best represent the Moiaimba community."

With barely a pause, the Member continued. "My colleagues are busy men and have commitments back in Port Moresby this afternoon so we'll proceed to sign the lease agreement while I host them to a small luncheon at the Guest Haus. Then we'll return to Moresby. Please come forward and sign your names here, and my representative will remain to make sure everything is in order. Thank you."

With that, the Member invited his guests to stand up and follow him out the door of the schoolroom and down to the Guest Haus. It was clear that he'd gagged the discussion and was not willing to take more questions. However what worried David and John and their colleagues now was whether there were enough Deria people present to gather the forty signatures required to allow the lease agreement to go through.

As soon as the Member and his party had left the room, Umbare David spoke up.

"Fellow Moiaimba clansmen, please give me your ears for a minute." He waited briefly until he had everyone's attention.

"We've just heard of this proposal to lease our land to host a gold mining venture here. This will have a huge impact on our community, with both positive and negative aspects. I believe that we need to have more time to understand these positive and negative aspects and how the future of our children and their children will be affected. We need help to do this.

"You're all aware that earlier this morning Justin Orlando was flown out after surviving a plane crash. For those who hadn't heard, Justin is a senior manager in the Department of Social Resources and had come to Mambusu a few days ago specifically to help us understand the impact of this Proposal. That's his job. He's the Mining Warden. He's already shown us these same plans that the Member has now just revealed. He explained many things about them to us.

"For my colleagues and I, it raised many more questions that we need answers to before we start leasing off our land to the company. The Member's lease scheme needs to be subject to legal scrutiny to make sure it's fully in accord with the Mining Act. We need time to make sure we are certain that this is in our best interests.

"I'm asking here for your restraint, and that you do *not* sign the Member's petition. At the same time I have prepared another petition that reads:

'As a member of the Moiaimba community, I wish to have more time and more information before considering leasing Mambusu land to Namel Mining Pty Ltd'.

"I apologise that it's only a handwritten paper because I've just prepared it now. But I ask you to sign this petition instead of the Member's to avoid us as a community finding ourselves committed to the land lease and mine before we are ready. Thank you."

David walked over to the table and placed his paper next to the Member's formal type written one. Paul motioned to David that he should stay and make sure the petition didn't disappear.

The Member's representative was aghast. How dare someone challenge the Member! He would make sure the Member was made aware of this as soon as he could.

As the last of the attendees left the room, only Paul and the Member's representative and their petitions remained. As best Paul could see there were quite a few names registered on the Member's list, but the representative quickly folded it over to avoid scrutiny. As Paul scrolled down through his own list he could see that he had at least thirty names there.

He wondered, when would they find out if the Member had gained the forty names he wanted?

Chapter 22

The Lunch

The visitors from South East Asia may not have spoken much English let alone Tok Pisin or Moi Tok Ples, but they could read faces and understand tone of voice. The Member could see that they too were raising some questions as they talked among themselves in their own language, and he wasn't happy about it. He'd assured the visitors that this signing was *fait accompli*, assured, except for the formality of getting the signatures. But what the visitors saw told a different story. They saw the dissent on the faces of at least half of those present. And it worried them.

So, as they sat down for their light lunch at the Mambusu Guest Haus, they had some questions for the Member. It was indeed a pity that Lily was not there to hear the exchange!

"Mr Walino," asked the spokesman and interpreter for the group, whose English was considerably better than the others, "can you tell me please, who is this Justin Orlando, is it?"

"Yes, Orlando I believe it is," replied the Member nonchalantly. "Yes, ah, he's just a government worker who came out last week to discuss the plans with the people here. I've never met him and you shouldn't concern yourselves with him. Actually the poor fellow was in a plane accident yesterday near here and nearly died. He was flown out to Port Moresby earlier today."

There was a pause while the spokesman discussed the response with his group.

"This Mr Orlando seems to have made some trouble for you, Mr Walino." The visitors were more perceptive than the Member may have realized, and had quickly picked up the vibes of discontent.

"Oh, I don't think he'll cause us any trouble gentlemen. As I said he's just a government worker doing his job, but he won't be involved any more. His injuries in the plane crash will mean he's off work for some time anyway."

Again, a pause, and discussion in their own language.

"Mr Walino, many of the people are not ready to sign up to lease their land. How do you explain that?" asked the spokesman. The Member was beginning to feel pushed by these people.

"Ah, it's just the normal process of negotiation. Believe me, this is what they really want. I've had many consultative meetings with them and so what you heard today was just one or two who are known as troublemakers in the community," replied the Member, starting to scratch for excuses.

"But do you call the Council President a troublemaker, Mr Walino?" It was obvious to the Member that the visitors were not lambs being led to the slaughter as he had presumed, but in fact highly intelligent professionals who'd done their homework for this trip. They were actually very well aware of who many of the people at the meeting were, and accurately gauged the mood of those present.

"We do not understand why the President had not seen the plans from you, Mr Walino." Again the spokesman was homing in on the Member. Did they already smell a rat?

"Gentleman, please, I've no idea why the President hadn't seen the plans. Perhaps he was out of the village when I made my visits? But I can assure you that the few people who were behind the President cannot change the course of the Proposal we have agreed to. As representative of the Moiaimba people, I speak for them. I know what their common voice is in this matter. So please relax and trust me. I know my people."

The Member hoped he'd said enough to convince the visitors. "So please, we have the pleasure of eating some local delicacies today, freshly harvested sago from just down the river, roasted in banana leaf with banana and pumpkin."

With that the Member made it clear he was going to enjoy his lunch. With his mouth now full of sago and banana anyway, he wasn't in a position to answer any more questions.

The visitors continued to discuss the situation vigorously in their own language, much more interested in their discussion than the sago and pumpkin roasted in banana leaf. As the meal came to an end, and the Member rose to indicate they should leave now to conclude the signing, he was interrupted by the spokesman.

"Mr Walino, we have decided that we are not ready to sign the land agreement. We are not satisfied that you have the full support of your people, and we must have that. But we have a request before we leave Mambusu?" he asked.

A little taken back at this delay, the Member nevertheless had no choice but to agree to their request. He motioned for them to speak.

"We wish to speak with the Council President briefly."

The Member was now starting to feel quite insecure and in fact realized that he was feeling quite hot and sweaty all of a sudden. It was nothing more than a mild panic attack, but one that he could do without.

"Ah, certainly gentlemen, would you like to wait while I get someone to bring him here?" suggested the Member.

"Perhaps we will go and find him ourselves, Mr Walino, and we like to walk around Mambusu to see the village more," replied the spokesman.

The situation was now growing quickly out of control for the Member and his level of discomfort was reaching extreme. But if he didn't give these men what they wanted, he would have little chance of getting what he wanted – the financial benefits from their mining venture.

Without waiting for him to reply, the spokesman thanked him, and the three of them walked out of the Guest Haus and into the village.

John Aitomo had walked back to his modest Council Offices after the meeting, and the three South East Asian visitors found him there easily. He greeted them as they entered the offices.

"Good afternoon gentlemen, welcome to the Mambusu Council Offices." Looking past them for signs of the Member, John asked, "Is the Member coming with you?"

"Good afternoon Mr President," said the spokesman politely, extending his hand. The other two men did the same and John warmly shook their hands. He didn't attempt to click fingers though. That was reserved for those in the inner circle of friends and relatives.

John was surprised that the Member was nowhere to be seen, a fact confirmed by the spokesman. "We have come by ourselves. We would like to ask you some questions, Mr Aitomo, if you do not mind?"

"Not at all, I'm very happy to answer your questions," replied John, secretly savouring this moment face to face with the visitors.

"We saw that there was some people like you who did not want to sign the land lease paper. Can you tell us why?"

John paused for a moment before replying. "Gentlemen, we've only heard of this Proposal in detail less than a week ago, through Mr Justin Orlando. His job was to come and discuss it with us and to help us understand all the aspects of the proposal that might affect us. He was very helpful to us, showed us the plans, walked to the proposed mine site area with us, and answered many questions for us. As Warden he is tasked by the government to conduct meetings with us.

"However we still have many questions to be answered, and so we're not ready to make a commitment to releasing our land yet. We need more time before we make that decision. I hope you can understand that?"

John had no reason not to be totally honest and open with these men whom he knew wanted to scoop up his land. He knew that effective negotiation could only happen in a climate of honesty.

The spokesman responded quickly, "But Mr Aitomo, Mr Walino has told us that he has visited many times to discuss the project with the people here. Is that not true?"

"It's not true gentlemen. The Member has not had a single meeting with the Mambusu community to discuss the Proposal, and even the community leaders haven't been informed about it. Only Mr Orlando has advised us of the project," replied John.

"If you have seen the plans from Mr Orlando then," the spokesman continued, "do you not feel you are ready to sign the lease agreement then? The Proposal is very good, ah? The benefit is very good for the Moiaimba people, ah?"

John now realized that this visitation from the visitors was an attempt to win him over. But he wasn't ready for that. So he'd have to shake them off.

"Gentleman, the Proposal is indeed very good, there's no doubt about that. Just as you have gone into every detail in your planning, so we as a community need to do our own planning. We've seen your plans but we haven't had time to discuss them together. That's how we do things in PNG, we discuss together in the wider community until we're all agreed on the course of action we wish to take. We'll advise the Member when we've come to a decision."

Before the visitors could respond to his comments, he began to usher them towards the door. "Thank you for your visit. It's a pleasure meeting you. I hope we meet again." He looked up at the sky. "The weather is closing in so I mustn't keep you from your helicopter trip back to Port Moresby."

With that he almost pushed them forward and down the road towards their helicopter. Almost as quickly he turned and walked back into his office. They had no chance to respond, and that was just what John wanted.

As soon as he saw the helicopter leave, in clear blue skies, John rounded up his colleagues to brief them on the discussion. Paul had the list of names that supported his petition, thirty-two in all. They were now sure that the Namel Mining company representatives were well aware that the Member didn't have the community support he may have promised them.

But the big unknown was still this – did more than forty people sign the Member's document? If they had, then the future of their land may already be decided.

Chapter 23

The Recuperation

Lily and I were able to fly back to Mambusu later in the afternoon, the same day I was discharged from hospital. I was confined to immediate bed rest under instructions from the doctors, enforced by Lily.

Grandfather's carved chair, which had suddenly assumed so much significance, came with me this time. However, I'd asked Lily not to mention it to anyone else. She'd wrapped it in old newspaper and taped around it to hide it from view as we travelled. I'd reveal it to the leaders at Mambusu when I was ready.

Kila had kindly taken us to the airport and used the opportunity during the drive to brief us on the latest developments with the Member.

"I think the Member is a little worried, Justin," reported Kila. "I hear that his trip to Mambusu didn't go as well as he'd hoped. He took three senior executives from Namel Mining, all Asians, with him. But it seems like he found some opposition to his ideas. I have a cousin who has an inside contact at Namel Mining headquarters at Six Mile. From what he's saying, the mining executives are suspicious that the Member isn't being transparent with them."

"Well, we all knew that," I replied, "The only question was how long it would be before Namel Mining realized it as well."

"Your friends in Mambusu will have more details," continued Kila, "but he tried to get enough people to sign a petition approving immediate lease of the land around Mambusu, you know, the same area as marked on the site map. It included all of the town plus up to about three kilometres all around it, and of course, the river junction up to the gold source. "

"Oh, wow." I was surprised. "I didn't expect Loopy would be so brazen at this stage. Buy out the community, eh?" I had to pause and think through what that might have involved. "There's not much about that side of things in the Proposal except that Namel Mining would control the land. Do you know how Loopy planned to make that happen? Would Namel lease it outright? Doesn't seem quite right to me." My mind was thinking through other mining developments I was familiar with.

Kila replied, "There'll be some scheme he has that'll make him rich, you can be sure about that. Actually I've been doing some research myself on some of the Member's financial activities."

"Ah, Detective Kila is on the job. Good work bro. Have you uncovered anything suspicious?" I asked.

"I think so," replied Kila. "He's been buying things on a cheque account called Moi Futures. I did a check at IPA and found it's a company with a single shareholder, a Mr L W Udio. I can't seem to get any more information on it than that. You might like to do some homework yourself when you get back to Mambusu. See if he's paid for anything there using that account, and if anyone knows who Mr Udio is." Kila was obviously a little frustrated that his search for more details had so far been fruitless.

"Ok, I'll keep that in mind," I said.

Lily, who was sitting in the back seat of the car, had kept silent while we talked.

"Boss," she suddenly said, and I was very aware of the term she'd just used to address me, "Udio is the Member's family name. It's the name of his grandfather. So L W Udio is him, Lupo Warina Udio. He's just used his grandfather's family name this time."

"Hey, that's also great detective work Lily. So it looks like he's tried to cover up his tracks by using his grandfather's name. The question now is, why?" I was enjoying this teamwork as we started to slowly unravel the Member's strategy.

"Kila, what happened with his bid to get the land lease approved at Mambusu? Did it work? Who controls the land now?" I asked.

"I don't have any details on that yet. He apparently needed forty signatories from landowners to approve the agreement. Some people signed up but I've no information on how many. By the sound of it there was some opposition voiced and that might have influenced a few people away from the idea."

"Ok then," I replied, "let me know when you get anything more on it."

Our helicopter flight back to Mambusu in good weather was uneventful, and that evening I was pleased to have my friends visit. Behind a closed door in my room at the Guest Haus, they debriefed me on the events while I was away. Slowly the pieces of the jigsaw were coming together. However the big question was still, did the Member gain more than forty signatures on his petition?

"Gentlemen," said John, "I believe that we have a duty to expose the Member. Even if he has gained the signatories he seeks, we need to expose him so that he's discredited. That way we can then look for a better way to proceed with the mine Proposal, one that genuinely includes community participation and the leadership of our people."

I thought it was time I now introduce some direction to the discussion.

"I've been reading my grandfather's diary recently, and find that he has some wisdom for us in this situation," I said. I was very aware that Lily was the only one in the group who knew who my grandfather was.

"I believe that we should be looking at this gold resource for what it can contribute to the community, rather than the profit it can make for the mining company and its shareholders at the expense of the community. So the starting point for us is to ask, 'what is the true value of the gold for the Moiaimba people?' If the gold cannot give back to us more than we already have, then we shouldn't be considering mining it."

My Mambusu friends paused with me. I knew they were struggling for answers to the gold mine question, and I could see them deep in thought at this new stream of thinking.

"Go on Justin, keep talking," said Hendros, the local businessman. I knew he'd understand some business sense.

"Well, the mining company is prepared to invest millions and millions of kina in developing its mine here. That's because it believes that there will be profits in the future, also millions and millions of kina. While there will be local people who gain wages and learn work skills, and there may be some new buildings put in here and there, there's a huge fortune to be made by the shareholders of the company. So my question is, if this is worth so much to them, why shouldn't it be worth at least that or more to us?"

Pausing for a minute to collect my thoughts, I realized I wasn't expressing myself as clearly as I wished, so I went on.

"What I mean is this, while they will gain a lot from their investment, whatever we gain will be at the expense of what we have to give up."

No one had appeared to notice that I was including myself and using the pronoun "we" as I spoke. I no longer thought of myself as an outsider, but was very aware that so far only Lily thought of me the same way.

"While the Member is obviously trying to gain some personal financial advantage through his dealings with the mining company, the greater question for us is whether we want this proposal to go ahead or not, and under what conditions. Or do we believe that we lose too much of our heritage, of who we are, that no amount of money can compensate for?"

I'd said enough for the moment. The leaders of Mambusu needed time to reflect. As they were preparing to leave, Lily approached my bed.

"Boss," she said quietly, "thought you should know that the Member paid for his lunch with a cheque from Moi Futures. Good night, and just ring this little bell if there's anything you need in the night. I'll be staying in the room next door." She pointed to a small bell with a wooden handle on my bedside table.

I was once again thankful for this intelligent and caring woman who had undertaken to look after me. With another week confined to bed while my foot and ankle began to heal, I'd need her care.

But at least I had a good book to read!

Chapter 24

The Dance

Grandfather continued his diary in high spirits over the next three months as he awaited the wedding ceremony. His diary entries focused from his prospects of marriage back again to his prospecting for gold. While he developed his gold digging upstream from the river junction, he also wrote of his life experiences. One particular incident caught my attention.

"*By now I seem to have gained acceptance in the community and so I find I am left on my own more frequently while my young attendants head back to the village. I have taken the time for more exploration in the jungle areas near my primary location, careful not to lose my bearings though.*

"*Yesterday I experienced the most majestic of displays the good Lord could have devised in nature.*

"*As I wandered into an area of the jungle I had not ventured into before, slightly inland of the river, I found myself, as usual, hot and sweaty. Being around midday, I lay down for a nap in amongst the moss and leaf litter. I must have slept for over an hour but was awakened by a scratching sound nearby. I turned my head and behold, just a few feet away in a small clearing, was a beautiful little bird doing a dance. It seemed to be picking up twigs and leaves in its beak to make the area clear as it strutted around.*

"*A small dark bird, either black or very dark blue, I could not discern due to the poor light in the jungle, it had several long stalks protruding from its head with what looked like feather balls on the end. I presume they are feathers. As the bird moved, these feathers bobbed around - quite mesmerising!*

"But then the bird began a most amazing dance. I presume it to be a courtship ritual. It was as if the bird turned itself inside out, and its dark feathers reversed somehow to become like a skirt around it. As it turned around and I saw it face to face, the most magnificent breastplate of colours became apparent. It was like jewels glistening vibrant colours of red, green, yellow, blue and purple. It outshone any rainbow I have ever seen and I was totally transfixed. The bird danced in a choreographed routine that only enhanced the bobbing of its head feathers, with coinciding flicking movements of its technicolour breastplate. This had the effect of changing the colours of the feathers. Any prospective mate in this display must be impressed! What a truly magnificent display I was treated to.

"Suddenly the bird was gone, darting back into the tree cover. I hoped it had found its mate. I lay on the jungle floor stunned by this performance, feeling so privileged to have seen it.

"Today when Seri returned, I told him of what I had seen, still absolutely enthralled by the display. His reaction was most unexpected. His face, even though dark skinned, almost went pale. His expression became serious and he looked quite stunned. He staggered back a little and then sat down on a log, staring at me.

"'Seri, are you ok?' I asked him in Moi language.

"He was silent. I was baffled by his reaction and could not understand at all why my story of the bird dance had shocked him.

"After a while he said to me, 'Adi, you must speak with my father.'

"With that Seri withdrew and kept himself aloof from me, as if he was fearful of me, or that there was now something

between us that had tempered his behaviour towards me. The jovial Seri had gone.

"I have no idea what has happened here and so I must get back to the village tomorrow to speak with Seri's father and get to the bottom of it. My relationship with the men has been seriously affected. I wonder if I have done something to upset the balance in my relationship with these people?

....

"Yesterday I was able to get up to the village. Seri's reaction was still foremost in my mind, and my total ignorance about its cause. His father greeted me when I arrived and escorted me with some reverence to meet with the elders. There was an air of seriousness that added to my own suspense now.

"The elders invited me to sit and then after some minor small talk to greet me, asked me to recount my story. I used Motu in places but found my Moi language ability adequate enough to describe much of the event. I did have trouble trying to describe the majesty and beauty of this magnificent little bird, but that did not detract from my description overall. From the nods and grunts offered by the elders at various stages of the dialogue, they were well familiar with the bird.

"No one spoke until I had completed my story. It was as if they also were captivated again by the magnificence of the bird and its plumage. Or was there something else that now entertained their minds? I was soon to find out.

"'Adi,' the headman addressed me. I looked up to see that it was none other than Seri's father. While I knew he was a leader in the village, I had no idea that he was actually the supreme chief of the tribe.

"'You have been among us for a wet season and half a dry season now. You have been welcome among us. You have made yourself known to us and we have come to accept your willingness to learn our customs and language. We have approved of your desire to marry a daughter of our tribe.'

"I knew this was not his main point. He was leading up to something else.

"Seri's father continued, 'There are many customs in our culture that are secret to us and you do not know them. They are secrets that we initiate our young men and women to, but not outsiders. Therefore we have kept these secrets from you. But it is now time for us to tell you these.'

"There was a pause as the elders looked around and quietly nodded approval to each other.

"'There's a legend in our ancestral stories that tells us that when the first members of our tribe entered this land, this land we now call Moi land, they were attacked along the way by coastal cannibals and many did not survive. Our stories tell us that these ancestors were from a coastal community many days sailing away. They were running out of food because of a drought and so some families decided to set off to find new land. One man did survive along with his wife and two small children. His name was Lupiano. They were able to flee up the Moi River from the coast and found themselves at the junction of the rivers. They moved further upriver and camped. One afternoon our ancestor father was resting in the jungle when he saw a beautiful small bird do a dance. It was the same bird that you saw.

"He took it as a sign that this was the place that the Creator God had chosen for him to live in peacefully with his family. We never talk about this bird or its dance so that we know that anyone who describes it must have seen it for themselves.

"However our tradition requires that future leaders of our clan will also only be people who have seen this little bird dance first hand. Because you have now seen the bird, then you have become an elder in our clan. That is why in our language we refer to the elders as 'nenge nematanu', 'the people of the bird'.'

"I was speechless. No wonder Seri was also shocked because he must have realized the significance of my story. I was describing something to him that was taboo, sacred, unspeakable, except for those who have seen it themselves.

Seri was now caught in a struggle by being exposed to something regarded as so secret in his culture. I felt for him and knew I would have to somehow help him through this.

"From being an intruder to becoming an elder in this society is nothing but a huge honour for me, so unexpected, but so precious. It is such a pity though that my honour is Seri's dishonour."

I put the book down on my lap as the significance of this began to dawn on me. I too had seen the bird, though no one else knew about it. I was glad I hadn't told Lily yet. In awe I reflected on how grandfather was guiding me now to understand my own journey with the Moiaimba, and with *nenge*.

I continued reading.

"The headman continued. 'The woman you have asked to marry is my daughter. It is our custom that the mantle of headman is passed to the first son of the headman's wife or of her daughter. Your status now as an elder of our clan marrying my daughter means that your son will become headman when I pass on to join the ancestors.

"'Adi, we welcome you to our inner circle of elders. To fully integrate you onto our culture and give you full acceptance into our community, we will proceed with initiating you as a Moiaimba.'

"I was amazed at how quickly these easygoing people were going to move ahead now to initiate me into their clan. I am still trying to understand how significant my marriage now to Leelak will be – that our son will become the tribal chieftain!"

Grandfather's mind was still whirling as he wrestled to come to grips with this new honour, as was mine as I contemplated my own situation. He continued to write about the initiation ceremony, which he thought the elders might have abbreviated for him! He did have to spend a couple of days living in the bush with a small group of other initiates, and then a full day ceremony of dancing and celebration, which continued well into the night around a huge fire.

The lights at the guest haus had gone out by now but my grandfather's story was so enthralling that I kept reading by the light of my torch. I read on as he survived the initiation rite of passage and prepared for his marriage to Leelak, still kept from seeing her until the day of the ceremony.

The wedding ceremony itself was traditional. PNG traditional, that is. No white dress and bridesmaids. No suits and ties. The Moiaimba dressed in simple coverings made of woven grass or light bark. The men with theirs tucked under a vine belt at the front and leaves of *tanket* shrub at the back. The women bare breasted with a woven skirt covering from waist to knees.

For the wedding the bride was covered in ceremonial *bilas*, ornaments such as cowrie shells, mother of pearl shells and colourful Bird of Paradise plumes. But no gold. There was a dowry exchange that had been agreed to by the elders, including grandfather. It consisted of a number of pigs and some gold which grandfather had persuaded Seri's father would enhance their future trading prospects in Port Moresby. Grandfather also wore traditional coverings, and both he and his bride were painted up with ochre colourings of red, yellow, light brown and black. It seems his western style clothing had worn out anyway!

After their marriage, grandfather was able to take his bride to live in his own house in the village – he had added extra rooms onto his one roomer. His love for Leelak shone through the penciled pages of his diary. Within a couple of months grandfather disclosed that Leelak was expecting their first child. The excitement in the village grew as they anticipated the next heir to the clan throne. Grandfather now wrote of his progress carving the rosewood chair, something that kept him active as he awaited the birth.

As much as grandfather may have wished that his wife could have given birth at a hospital that offered modern day health services, this birth was to be just another village delivery. The village midwives had been coaching Leelak in the months leading up to the birth, and grandfather was kept in ignorance about much of it. This was women's business and men had no part of it.

"My dear Leelak is going in to labour and so the time of delivery is rapidly approaching. I fear for her safety in these primitive conditions yet have a confidence because so many others have gone through this ritual of childbirth and survived. The midwives have gathered with her in the house prepared for her. I am not allowed to be within proximity and will be advised when the birth is completed.

.....

"After half a day of labour, my darling has delivered us a beautiful little girl. It is not usual to give a child a name for several weeks because there is such uncertainty about it surviving. The women have brought her in to meet me. She has the most gorgeous little face, and her skin is quite light and pink. God has blessed me with this little one. I cannot wait to share her with my dear wife."

The great intrigue in reading a diary, and one so personal as this, is that it captures the emotions of the moment. As the author writes, there is something of the heart that is transferred to ink, the translation of intimate feelings to written words, and the joy, the pain, the excitement and pathos is captured in an instant of time. Each entry paints a different picture. Each new day is a fresh canvas, and the events it brings give the artist writer a new palette of emotional colours.

So it was that as I read on, my grandfather was plunged from total joy to utter despair.

"My worst fears have been realized and I am in utter despair. I have waited since the birth of our beautiful little one yesterday until today to see my beloved Leelak. But today her father has come with tears himself to inform me that during the night she perished. The reason is unknown and I have not seen her. I have not said goodbye. In the exercise of childbirth, she has given her life. The village has commenced a period of mourning. I have never felt so alone and so much in despair."

My torch wavered and blacked out.

Chapter 25

The Unveiling

The next day was to be one of my most significant at Mambusu. I decided that I'd reveal my identity to the Mambusu leaders. With the rosewood chair now in my room, my plan was to unwrap it, invite them in, and see their reactions. Then I'd let the conversation take its course.

As I gazed at the chair once more, a swell of emotion almost overwhelmed me as I recalled the despair that had now engulfed my grandfather at the loss of his dear Leelak. I took a few minutes to let the grief pass, then called Lily in to share my plan.

But first I needed to confirm more of Lily's story, so I cautiously asked her, "Lily, can you tell me a little more about your grandfather's sister? Am I correct in saying that she died in childbirth, and gave birth to a daughter?"

Lily turned her gaze from me for a moment, paused, and then with tears ready to swell in her eyes, said a simple "Yes."

"And can you tell what happened to the little girl? It's important that I know this, please trust me even though I know this is very personal to you," I asked.

Once again Lily paused for moment, then replied in a soft voice, "I can tell you. The prospector took her soon after and went back to his place with her. We never heard anything more about her." It was clear that there was a deep sense of communal grief all these years later. Did the Mambusu people regard grandfather's act as kidnapping?

I too was somewhat emotional at this news, but it explained the link that had been missing in my mind until now.

"Lily," I gently continued, "thanks for telling me this. I'm going to tell you something now that's very important to me, and you are the first person to know this." I paused as I chose my words. "The gold prospector was my grandfather. I know that from his diary. I believe the little girl, his daughter, is my mother."

There was silence for several minutes as we both let our minds come to grips with this truth.

"The chair," she suddenly exclaimed, "that explains why you have the chair! You must be The One then. You are her son. If the headman's wife's firstborn child is a daughter, then the mantle of leadership passes to the daughter's firstborn son. That's you!!"

The tears streamed down her face. Without a second thought she reached out and threw her arms around me, her excitement hardly containable.

After she'd settled back to earth again, I shared my plan with her, and she agreed with it. With the speed at which events were taking place with the gold mine proposal, it was best to reveal all as soon as possible. She'd arranged a meeting for 10 am. Carefully she unwrapped the chair, reliving its unveiling to herself just a day earlier, chuckling as she worked. For my part, there were too many convergent signs for me to have any doubt about my Moiaimba past, or my Moiaimba future!

As each of the group, John, Paul, Hendros and David entered the room, I watched their faces carefully. None of them spoke as they saw the rosewood chair and moved to take up their assigned seats squeezed around my bed. Lily was the last one in. There was silence for a few minutes before David spoke.

"Justin, this chair," he motioned, pointing to it with his chin, "…where did you get it from?"

"Why do you ask, David?" I replied, hoping to explore a little more of their folklore before revealing mine.

"We didn't expect to see this chair. Not anywhere. Especially not here in Mambusu. There are stories about it, but we didn't expect ever to see it. It belongs in our past." He paused, and looked at his colleagues. They too were deep in reflection, too deep to be able to say much.

"Can you tell me about these stories?" I asked.

"You're a visitor here, an outsider. You're not part of our people and so it's very hard for us to disclose these stories to you." He knew I was seeking an entrance to know deeply held clan secrets. He turned to his fellow elders and they talked together in Moi language.

"We're confused now," continued David, "to find this chair in your room with you. All we can tell you is that this chair matches the description of one that has great meaning in our cultural traditions. We can only presume it's the same chair. The carvings are of things only the elders of the Moiaimba know about. We must know how you got the chair."

I realized that I must now give them more information to gain their confidence.

"I need to tell you two stories," I began. "The first is about an Australian gold prospector. In the early 1920's he made his way up the Moi River to the junction in search of gold. He quickly made friends with the local people, and in time married one of the women in Mambusu. Her name was Leelak. Her father was the headman in the village…" I was just about to say 'whose name was Lupiano' but stopped.

Another piece of the jigsaw had fallen into place in my mind, one that should have been evident long before now. I'd thought Lupiano to be an Italian giveaway but now realized how wrong I'd been. This name was passed down to the headmen of Mambusu from the first family who established themselves here. Lupiano was not a name, it was in fact a title. It was the headman's title.

After a few moments in thought, I looked up to see my friends waiting for me to continue. Obviously my story had captivated them.

"I'm sorry," I said, "I just realized something quite important. Where was I? Yes, the headman's daughter. She gave birth to a child, a girl, but unfortunately died during childbirth. The gold prospector was distraught and left Mambusu soon after, taking his daughter with him.

"In the time between his marriage and the birth of their child, the prospector made a chair from rosewood, this chair. He listened to the tribal stories and made carvings around the chair reflecting some of those stories. When he left Mambusu, he told the people that the person who returns with the chair will be their next headman."

So far I'd deliberately told them nothing that linked me directly to the prospector, except of course that the chair was now in my possession. In part I wanted them to make those linkages.

"The second story is my own experience while I was in the bush waiting to be rescued…" I hesitated. "Lily, I'll have to ask you to leave us while I tell this story."

I hated to have Lily leave the room, but I didn't want her to be inflicted with the same curse that Seri had come under.

I continued. "I dragged myself away from the aircraft in case it caught fire. As I lay in the undergrowth, I saw a beautiful sight. A small black bird was cleaning a little area of forest floor, picking up twigs and leaves. When it was finished, it started to do a dance. This was the most beautiful sight I've ever seen. The bird had long feathers coming out of its head that bobbed around as it danced. But it seemed to turn its body feathers inside out so that it looked like it was wearing a skirt. That's the carving on the front of the chair legs here." I pointed to the carvings on my chair legs.

"The most beautiful part of the bird though was its breastplate, which sparkled with the colours of the rainbow as it danced, flipping from side to side. All too quickly the bird was gone but I'll remember its dance for as long as I live."

My friends were now entranced. I had revealed to them the most sacred of tribal experiences. An outsider just minutes ago, I'd revealed to them not just a story of seeing a beautiful bird, but the unveiling of a prophecy that was held sacred by their tribe. Not only did I know their secret, but was I also the fulfillment of the gold-miner's prophetic word? I could see this question on each of their minds, reflected on their faces.

I asked for Lily to join the group again, and continued, "I hope that I can in time tell you the full story, but at the moment it's enough for me to tell you this. The prospector is my grandfather. His daughter is my mother."

The men sat before me stunned, speechless, eyes wide.

As if to remove any doubt to my heritage, I added, "My grandfather left me this chair when he died, along with a diary he wrote about his time at Mambusu. I knew nothing of this story until a few weeks ago. The only thing that I did know, though I had no idea of its meaning, is that he insisted that I be given a particular name at birth." I paused for effect.

Lily spoke it first, very softly but with an intensity of awe and respect.

"Lupiano," she whispered.

I couldn't help but notice the smile on her face as she watched the men's reaction.

After what seemed like an eternity of silence, David spoke.

"I have a question for you. Have you ever visited Mambusu before you came last week?" he asked, his mind still deep in reflection about what I'd just revealed.

"Actually, yes. I first visited Mambusu in 1972. I was winger in a representative schoolboys' rugby team that visited. We came to Mambusu for one night and played a game of football here," I answered.

"How well do you remember that visit?" asked David again. I was certainly surprised that after telling my story of the chair and seeing the bird, let alone revealing that I was their next headman, that they'd be more interested in any earlier visits I may have made.

"Well to tell you the truth, that trip to Mambusu changed my whole life," I replied. "I still remember leaving and feeling like I'd left part of my heart behind here. It was because of that night here that I decided that my future was in PNG. It was because of the needs I saw as you approached Independence as a community still emerging into the modern world, and the sense that I could offer something to help, that I returned to PNG. I really don't know why it took me so long to get back here to Mambusu though!"

David was staring at me seriously, and I thought his eyes were going to pierce right through me.

"Do you remember me?" he asked, still staring at me.

"Umbare David…. David Umbare, yes, I do know you. I knew your name was somehow familiar. I do… you were the teacher who told me about life here and patiently answered my questions. Yes, now I remember you."

If it hadn't been for my leg, I would have jumped up and hugged him. The memory came back fresh and clear now as if it was yesterday. As it was, a huge smile spread across David's face and he jumped up and embraced me as I lay on the bed.

"Justin, the story you've told us doesn't surprise us. The story of your grandfather and his chair, and his daughter, are legends in our culture. There are one or two of our older men and women who were very young at the time but remember your grandfather. His memory has been kept alive for one reason particularly."

David paused and looked at me, as if to say that I already knew why.

"Because his daughter's son would be the next headman?" I ventured to suggest.

"For someone who was an outsider a week ago, you have a very good knowledge of our cultural stories and prophesies!" exclaimed David. "Tell me, you didn't learn those from me in 1972. Where did you learn them?"

So I told them about the diary.

"My grandfather had a diary in which he kept a record of his daily activities during his time in PNG. After he passed away and left me the chair, I started to restore it. While doing that I found the diary hidden in the seat of the chair in a rosewood pocket. It had been hidden all this time." I reached into the drawer of my bedside table and lifted out the diary for them to see. "He never talked of his PNG time. No one in the family even knew of it. Perhaps the memories were too painful?" David's question had, as he no doubt intended, opened me up to share more of the story.

I continued, "I never knew my mother was half Papua New Guinean. She had a darker complexion than most Australians of course but this was just her and we never even noticed her skin colour. We never knew her history either. I guess she was just a baby when grandfather arrived back in Australia and she grew up as an Australian. She's an old lady now. I don't even know if she knew her history. It seemed to be a secret that grandfather kept, except he knew it was in his dairy.

"Anyway, to answer your question, he wrote down many of the stories he heard as well as his own experiences seeing the bird and marrying Leelak."

The men and Lily listened intently. I was aware that the bond between us had deepened significantly. I was no longer an outsider.

"What has surprised us is the manner in which you have been brought back to Mambusu," said David thoughtfully. "With the coming of the gold mine, we have realized that we need the leadership of a strong, wise and compassionate headman again. Our political leader, the Honourable Member, is not that man. In our traditional stories we've always believed that this headman will come back to lead us through a time of great upheaval and crisis. We're now clear that you are that man. There's no doubt in our minds that you are Lupiano."

David finished what he was saying with a clear sense of finality. The others nodded their heads in agreement.

I waited in case David had more to say, but what more was there to say? I'd revealed my credentials, and now the leaders of the village had accepted them. I was Lupiano, the new headman.

"Gentlemen and Lily, I'm overwhelmed at the moment. I came here less than a week ago in the hope of helping this community understand the implications of the mine. This is the same motivation that has been behind all that I have sought to do in my working life here in PNG.

"But the events of the last week, revealed to me through my grandfather's diary, make it clear that I've come home. I've discovered my heritage, my family, and my calling to serve my people here."

I paused as I considered carefully what I would say next. They were words I had pondered and rehearsed in my mind since seeing the bird.

"My life is now here in Mambusu leading my people into the future. I feel deeply honoured that you, the leaders of Mambusu, have accepted me in that role. I'm proud to be one of 'the people of the bird', *nenge nematanu*. I'm proud to be Lupiano."

As I mouthed those words, an intense sense of pride swelled up within me, and a joy that was unspeakable. I felt like dancing! Oh how I wished I could jump out of bed and dance on two legs!

"Justin, from now on we will call you Lupiano, for that is who you are. We too feel the pride you feel at becoming one of us, *nenge nematanu*. We have a sacred dance that we, the *nenge nematanu* , perform when we're together. It's secret to our small group of elders."

I suddenly realized that Lily was still here in the room with us. David must have seen me glance over to her and the momentary flash of concern across my face. She wasn't part of the *nenge nematanu*. Yet David was revealing secrets never before shared with those who were not *nenge nematanu*, especially a woman.

"I notice that you are rightly concerned about Lily's presence here with us, and that she's not an initiate into the *nenge nematanu*. That concern for our tribal heritage is the mark of a leader," said David. He paused in reflection then continued.

"But times are changing. The world is different now. The place of women is becoming accepted. Lily has proved herself in the community as a leader among us even though she is not *'nenge nematanu'*. So we approve of her witnessing the customs of the *'nenge nematanu'* without fear or hesitation."

With that the four men stood up, locked arms through their elbows, and started to dance around my bed. At first I was confused. It looked like they were doing a Scottish Highlands jig. But then I saw it. They were mimicking the dance of the little black bird as it bobbed up and down, flicking from side to side.

I began to realize how much this beautiful little bird had infiltrated Moiaimba society. How it had become so important to the people. How the leadership of this society actually depended on the bird to nominate its leaders. Since the first sighting by the original settler family, it had become a mystical figure in Moiaimba culture, revealing itself only to those destined to become leaders. Was it even the same bird that kept revealing itself to generation after generation? The little bird had created a mythology around itself that was now a central source of identity for these people. The aura of *'nenge nematanu'* was such a powerful force for cohesion within this society, it was no wonder that in language and customs the bird was so honoured and held as sacred. Without the bird, the Moiaimba were nothing.

The dancing stopped, the men puffing and out of breath but absolutely full of life. Their new joy was infectious and I was feeling invigorated by it.

"Let us tell you a story now," said David, who had assumed the role of spokesman this night.

"We also have stories about you from your visit in 1972. Some of us remember you and felt a bond with you on that visit. We didn't know then what we know now about you. But we hoped that one day you'd return. The reason it's taken you so long is because the time was not right for you to return. We are Christian people now who believe that God has a time for these things to happen. We also see that our traditions say the same thing. You came when the time was right."

David continued, "There's something else which we can reveal to you now. For many years we, the leaders and our relatives, have believed that one of our daughters was best suited to be the wife of the next Lupiano. So while we didn't say much to this person or disclose this to her, we've held her back from marriage until the next Lupiano was revealed to us."

My heart rate was increasing rapidly. The leaders had already marked out a wife for me!! Suddenly I felt overwhelmed, of being locked into something I wanted but didn't want. Suddenly I was now being expected to adhere to the leaders' demands on my personal life. I felt that I was suffocating.

David and the others must have felt my sudden rise in apprehension and decided to put me out of my misery quickly.

"Yes, we've seen the bond between you and Lily over the last few days, and it's only confirmed to us our own judgment on the matter. Lily is the person we chose to be the Lupiano's wife. She is the one we wish you to marry."

From a mountaintop of apprehension, my spirit soared into the heavens with relief and joy. I looked at Lily. Her surprise was also complete. Her hands both went up to cover her mouth, opened wide with shock. But I could still see her eyes, also wide open, and in them I could see her joy as well.

Chapter 26

The Strategy

It was appropriate that there was a formal recognition of the relationship between Lily and I, and the village leaders in their wisdom recognised this. The intimacy that Lily and I would share while she attended to me during my recuperation demanded it. It would not otherwise be appropriate for a single woman to be giving that level of attention to a single man alone and in private.

We did make one break with village protocols though, with the elder's agreement. Lily and I would not be banned from seeing each other before the wedding ceremony. Perhaps my broken leg was a blessing in disguise because the announcement of our engagement and her need to be able to care for me sanctioned this change in custom.

Over the next two weeks I spent more and more time getting up and around on my crutches, so that by week three after the accident I felt comfortable enough to no longer be restricted to my bed.

For the first few days after getting back to Mambusu, even after the briefing on the first night back, I didn't really think much about the gold mine, and no one else mentioned it. I think people just wanted me to enjoy the rest. It gave Lily and I a chance to talk about the future.

On day four though I received a phone call from Kila.

"Hey Justin, good to hear your voice," he greeted me, "hope you're enjoying the break. I hear some good news on the grapevine too…"

"Who's been leaking my secrets?" I replied in a jovial spirit. I had no doubt that news of my engagement to Lily would travel fast. I wondered if Kila also knew of the rest of the story, and that he was now talking with the new headman?

"Congratulations bro, I can only say it's taken you a while, but I think Lily and you will make a great couple. How's your leg going?"

"Not too bad, I'm just starting to get an hour or two each morning and afternoon on my feet, or should say on my foot. I'm not in any real pain now," I replied.

"That's really good news Justin," said Kila, and continued, "Hey, thought I'd ring you with some news from Namel Mining, not good I'm afraid. It seems that the Member is claiming forty one names on his list and wants now to proceed with lease of the land for the mining company."

Kila paused so I could take in what he'd just said.

"I haven't thought much about the mine for a few days, so thanks for jolting me back to reality, bro," I responded in a joking tone of voice.

"I think whatever the real result was," I continued, "it was always going to be more than forty. It doesn't worry me too much because I suspected this. Can you get hold of a copy of the Member's list so we can go through all the names carefully? We need to make sure all are genuine names of people who were in attendance at the meeting, and that all are genuine landowners of the land indicated on the mine map. We only need to find two names that are rigged to make the Member's lease plan invalid."

"Yeah, I thought you'd ask for that so I've got my contacts trying to get a copy of the list as we speak. It'll be hard to get our hands on but I've directed that we need the document available for our Department lawyers to confirm the legality of any arrangements prior to issue of a mining lease. I'll let you know when I have it," said Kila. Once again I was impressed with his desire to bend over backwards to assist.

"Oh, by the way," Kila continued, "when do I put a date in my diary? The kids are already excited about meeting Aunty Lily!"

"Give us a few weeks or even months bro," I said, "I need to get on my feet first. But you'll be the first to know."

"Ok, my kids will hold you to your word. I might even have a pig or two I can contribute as well!" replied Kila. I deeply appreciated his generosity, totally oblivious to the irony of the offer.

It was time to call the troops together and so Lily called around to arrange a meeting with the leaders that afternoon. My rosewood chair had been transferred to the main room of the Guest Haus now, where it had become the pride of the village. It was quite common to find some of the village people gathered around it deep in discussion. For the meeting though, I sat in the chair with my feet up on a carved Sepik stool.

"I've received word from my boss that the Member is claiming that he has forty-one names on his paper," I advised the group. "I find that hard to believe given that we have thirty two names on ours and by all indications there were no more than sixty people at the meeting. I've asked Kila to try and get a copy of the list so we can verify every name as a genuine landholder in Mambusu and attendee at the meeting. I think our best plan at the moment is to try and get that list to below forty names."

"Lupiano, I agree with you," said Hendros. "I reckon that some of those names will be landowners from Deria but not here where the mine is proposed."

"And I wonder if the Member himself and his team have entered their names?" queried John, "because I don't think he's a landowner here."

"Yes, that's right," said Lily, "his family are landowners further up the mountain from Deria, so they're not eligible to be on the list." It was clear that Lily had been doing some homework on the Member's assets.

I continued, "I think we should continue with our campaign on the basis that we'll find a way to negate the Member's lease plans. We do need to know in our own minds whether we want this land lease and the mine to go ahead or not. That is still a fundamental question for us. But in the meantime, we should proceed as if the land lease and mine proposal are not going ahead. In other words, what options are there for us if we don't accept the mine proposal?"

David spoke up now, "Things have moved way too fast for us with this proposal, and that's been part of the Member's strategy - to push it through while we're still in ignorance. That way he expects us to say yes to everything he says because we haven't had opportunity to consider the options. Lupiano, I think you have given us good direction here. We need to slow the Member down and make sure we've considered all options for our community. The gold has never been an attraction for us. But we're now at a crossroads where we must recognise it as something that will be a blessing or a curse to us in future. It's something that we now have to recognise as valuable, and determine what that value is for our people."

Lily spoke up again. "I've been going through the plans that Justin, I mean Lupiano…" she paused, "I'm confused, what should I call you?" She looked up at me as she finished her question.

David spoke up quickly, "Daughter, it's good that you show respect to our brother as headman, especially in public, so it's appropriate that you call him Lupiano. When you're together in private, then you'll decide together what terms you use to refer to each other."

"Thank you, Elder-uncle," replied Lily, glad to have that matter cleared up.

She continued, "As I was saying, I've been going through the plans and trying to get some idea of a comparison of profits against expenses for the mine. I think the figures are probably deliberately downplayed but they still indicate a profit of 25 million kina a year on average. That means the 15% share which would come to the Namel Community Trust is 3.75 million kina per year."

Hendros, the businessman interrupted. "So if we could find an alternative to the mine that gave us an income of over 3.5 million kina a year….. but without losing our land…."

"That's exactly what I'm thinking," replied Lily. "Not only do we not lose our land but remember that the mine site will bring a huge amount of destruction to our area. Our gardens and the river will be affected. Just look at the Fly River and the destruction caused by the Ok Tedi mine. We don't want that happening to our river system."

"You're right, Daughter," interjected Paul, "and I don't trust the mining company to hold to their word either. As I read these plans, the alternatives they are suggesting for tailings dam and shipment of the ore down river are good ideas, but nothing more. As far as I can see, none of the methods they are proposing have actually been used elsewhere in the world."

It was John's turn to speak again. "I'm uncomfortable with the attitude of the mining company. As you know, I believe they're very aware of the Member's manipulation of the situation here at Mambusu, and so don't trust him. But when the Asian directors came to see me after the Member's meeting, I first thought they were on the same side as us. But it quickly became very clear that they were only interested in securing the land and getting their mine operating. Despite their sweet talk and deals, I'm not convinced that our interests will be respected."

"So let's sum up the situation as we see it so far," I said, taking advantage of a pause in the conversation. "We know the Member has been manipulating things to try and get the land lease done. In fact, he may even be out of order by trying to facilitate landowner arrangements prior to the Warden's hearing. The Mining Act does state a clear process to be followed in these negotiations.

"He's been using an account called Moi Futures to pay for things, and while we know that he's listed as sole Director, we know nothing more about that company. We also know that there's a trust fund called Namel Community Trust of which the Member is Chairman, and Namel Mining is the parent company."

"Yes, and that the 15% dividends will be paid into the Namel Community Trust fund according to the Member, but how much will actually end up in community hands?" added Hendros.

"Ok, good," I replied. "We also have the plans for the proposed mine, and while the Member is claiming he has the landowner signatures needed to release the Mambusu and mine site land, we're investigating that claim. In the meantime we're looking at other options that recognise the value of the gold but also recognise the cost to us if the mine goes ahead.

In financial terms, we think that we need an alternative that will return three and a half to four million kina annually in profits for the community, but without the loss of habitat for us. Does that sound about right to everyone?" I asked.

Lily nodded but added, "Except that if there's no destruction of our land and ongoing maintenance costs associated with that, we can accept much less than four million kina year."

"Could you to follow up on some legal details as well thanks Lily?" I asked. "I think Namel Mining has an Exploration License which is due to expire soon. Kila will have the details that I didn't bring with me. I guess that may be one reason why they're in a rush to get the lease approval underway, so they can make way to convert this to a Mining Lease. So we need to find out exactly what their tenement status is in case we can use that to our advantage. The other thing we need to check in more detail is on what basis the Minister will reserve an area from mining under Section 7 of the Mining Act."

Lily nodded as she took notes of my request.

"One more thing I think we must note as well," said David. "The Member comes from Deria village up the mountain, and there has always been traditional rivalry between Deria and Mambusu. He's already tried to use his Deria supporters to gain the upper hand in the private meeting. So we shouldn't underestimate the power of his lobbying. For the Deria people the mine would be fantastic – lots of benefits. But they don't have to sacrifice their land."

"Wise words, Elder-brother," I responded to David. "We don't want the Member to trap us again."

"I have one more comment," I said as we prepared to conclude our meeting.

"You've been part of my journey over the last two weeks. I came to Mambusu as a government employee to assist this community prepare for transition to a mining community. My primary official role was as Warden. But I'm now a different person. I've experienced a re-birth. I now have the interests of this community as my only responsibility. I'm preparing my resignation from government service and from now on I'm totally committed to my Moiaimba people."

There was a moment of silence as the group looked at me. Then one by one they began to applaud. They had no doubt now that they had my total allegiance. Lupiano had come home.

Chapter 27

The Crosses

Kila called me two days later. He had a copy of the Member's list of names and was driving up that afternoon to spend a few days at Mambusu. While he could easily justify this as part of his job, he wanted to help us go through the list of names. I thought he seemed keen to be part of the team.

"You should know that the Member has had his lawyers draw up the Lease Contract for the land. I suggest we need to move quickly or the transaction will be concluded," he said.

"Bro, is there any name on that list that you have doubts about? If we can find even one name then we can seek a stay until the list is verified," I suggested.

"To be honest Justin, I don't know any of these names. The first one is barely legible and the last one looks like Upio or Udio W. Again, the last one is barely readable as well," said Kila.

Something rang a bell in my mind. "Hang on, just say that last name again… isn't Udio the Member's family name?" I asked.

"Yes, you're right. He used his name as L W Udio on the Moi Futures account, and looks like he has used Udio W. to add a name to the list," replied Kila.

"I think we're onto something here Kila," I said. "Lily told us that all the Udio family land holdings were uphill from

Deria village and not at all within the land indicated on the mine Proposal. So whether that is the Member or not, the Udio family are not landowners in our area."

I smiled. I was sure I could almost hear Kila smiling at the other end of the phone as well!

"Can you apply for an immediate court injunction to stop any further proceedings with the land lease until we can verify the validity of the Member's list of landowner names?" I asked excitedly. We both felt it. The Member may not have been careful enough and cracked the door open for us to stop his scheme. "If that doesn't work, we may be able to look at other legal options. Any agreement between the company and landholders about compensation must come to a Warden's meeting. But let's try knocking him out before that."

"I'll get onto that absolutely immediately. I'm already halfway out the door to my car so I'll head straight to Waigani. I'll give you a call when I'm ready to leave Moresby to drive up." Kila hung up and I quietly wished him well with the court order.

Two hours later I received the call from Kila. He'd been successful in gaining an injunction, and the Member was restrained for a week. That means we had a week to come up with a verification of his list and be able to prove it didn't meet the required forty signatories.

Kila arrived on sunset and I welcomed him to Mambusu. We enjoyed a hearty meal and relaxed evening at the Guest Haus, with Lily's company as well of course.

"Wow, what a beautiful valley this is," commented Kila at one stage. "The drive up here is absolutely beautiful. The river is majestic and I really enjoyed driving up the winding road once I left the coast. It seems to play hide and seek with the river."

I needed to inform Kila of my new status as headman, and give him my resignation. So rather than prolong things, I decided to do it that evening as we talked.

As I told him my story, except for the bird sighting of course, his eyes grew gradually wider and wider. By the end of it, he was flabbergasted. Then I advised him that with my new home and status, I was resigning from the Department of Social Resources and would be leading the Moiaimba through their decision on the mine.

"Oh, wow," was about all Kila could say at first. But then he realized the situation I was now in and confirmed that I was doing the best thing for the Moiaimba. Of course, gaining a wife as part of the deal was a bonus!

"Justin, or should I call you Lupiano now? Whatever. I want to let you know that I'll support you in whatever you are going to do here. We both know that we're fighting political corruption here as well as deciding what the right thing for your people is. As Chief Warden, I'll also personally take over the Warden role."

Kila continued. "I've seen, as you have, how gold fever affects people. Politicians become greedy, landowners lose sight of their responsibility for their land, community leaders think that money to buy Landcruisers is all that matters. But I've come to believe that in many ways our people are being led astray, and in the process are losing their most valuable assets – their land and their culture. This is the heritage that God has given us, and no mining company or government has the right to take it away.

"I too was led into a trap by the Member, and I'm embarrassed to say that I fell into it. I've asked forgiveness from the Lord, and God has released me from the guilt of it. If it's found out, I could lose my job and face the courts. But I've found a new strength to fight this political corruption. So

I want you to know that I'm willing to assist you in any way I can to make sure the Member is brought to justice."

I was surprised to hear this confession from Kila, but it did start to explain why he'd been so helpful over the last few weeks. Once again I appreciated the friendship of this colleague, who would be invaluable as part of the team.

The next day I woke up with birds on my mind. Not any birds, just the little black one, *nenge*. I must have been dreaming about it again. The remembrance of its sparkling technicolour breastplate was so fresh. But in my dream, its breastplate was only one colour, gleaming gold. Its beauty so beguiling, I lay in bed just reliving my sighting of it once again.

We'd decided to take Kila down to visit the land in the junction and walk as far as we could up to the gold source, to give him a firsthand feel for the land. The weather was good and Lily packed some refreshments for the day. I couldn't go of course, being on crutches, so David, Hendros and John went with him. It would be a good chance for them to talk together about the mine proposal without me, for a change.

Lily stayed with me at the Guest Haus and we decided to do some brainstorming about alternatives to the gold mine given the parameters we'd discussed earlier.

Lily suggested we lie out the maps once again on the table and see if that gave us any ideas.

"Let's look at these maps closely and see exactly where the land they want is. Perhaps we'll have some inspiration from that?" she suggested.

We started with the Mambusu area, and carefully traced our fingers around the borders, noting where the village was now and where buildings were projected for the future. We noted where it led into corridors for transport and up to the airstrip, around the airstrip, and a section that led down the hill to the river junction.

No inspiration so far.

Pulling out the second map that contained the actual mine site, we did the same thing. Tracing the border of the land required by Namel Mining, we followed the riverbanks up from the junction then into an expanded area around the gold source, and back down to the junction.

Still no inspiration.

We stared at the maps for a while, wondering what to do next. For no apparent reason I said to Lily, "Here's the gold source, it runs for about 100 metres from the river inland here." I had a pencil in my hand and drew a line where the gold vein ran.

Without a thought, I decided to also mark the place where the aircraft crashed.

"Here's where the aircraft crashed," I said to Lily as I drew an X on the map.

"Here's where I found you on the riverbed," said Lily, and she took the pencil from my hand and marked another X on the riverbank.

To our astonishment, the Xs sat right next to the gold line. The aircraft had crashed within metres of the gold vein, and I'd been picked up still within metres of it.

"Wow, I crashed right into the gold," I said. "I didn't realize that was where we were though I knew Mitch flew us back up from the junction. That's amazing!"

Another thought occurred to me. It was very clear. 'Draw on the map where you saw the bird dance.'

I couldn't recall my movements exactly, so I didn't really know which direction I moved to get away from the aircraft or to slide down to the river. But by logically projecting what I could recall, I traced from the river and aircraft to a point on the map, and marked another X.

"This is where I thought I saw the bird, *nenge*, Lily. I haven't told you much about that but will do one day," I explained to her.

"But that's right on top of the gold vein, Justin!" she exclaimed, pointing to where my X intersected with the gold line. I looked closer at the map.

"You're right," I replied, "the bird dance place and the gold vein are exactly the same location. Wow!"

Now we were inspired!

"Lily, now I understand what my dream was about last night. The *nenge* was warning me. You know that the *nenge* is the most important cultural icon the Moiaimba have. It's everything to them. But nenge's home and the gold source are the same place. *Nenge* is the real gold for the Moiaimba.

"But if the gold mine goes ahead, it'll destroy the *nenge*, and that will destroy the Moiaimba".

Chapter 28

The Departure

With all that had happened since I boarded Mitch's Cessna, I'd forgotten about grandfather's diary. It was where I'd left it, in the desk drawer in my room at the Mambusu Guest Haus. The decision to not take it on the flight had been a wise one as it may not have been retrieved undamaged from the aircraft and be lost forever.

Lily and I packed up the maps with the realization that the mine could not proceed. To do so would be suicide for the Moiaimbu. I decided to spend the afternoon reading grandfather's diary again, at least until Kila and the team returned, which would probably not be until later in the afternoon, approaching sunset.

When I last read the diary, grandfather had been plunged into despair by the death of his wife, Leelak. Lily had told me that he'd left Mambusu soon after and taken his baby daughter with him. I was suddenly eager to hear from him again.

There was silence in his pages for a few days after his last entry, then he picked up his pencil again to continue the saga.

"It is now four days since Leelak passed away in the aftermath of giving birth. I have not known such despair and sorrow possible as I have these past days. But I am grateful when the village women bring my darling little daughter over and I can hold her in my arms. She has the most

gorgeous complexion and such lovely brown eyes. I see her mother in every move she makes.

"The women have found a foster mother who is breast feeding my little one. The care for one another within this society is wonderful. They have extended that to me as well, and there are constantly people with me in the house. They refer to it with a special vocabulary, and the best I can translate it is 'cry house' or 'house cry'. It seems to refer to the event of bereavement as well as the actual house where the bereaved gather. Food is always made available to me though I have had little inclination to eat.

"My loved one was laid to rest yesterday, after three days. I was able to see her beautiful face for the last time. In fact, she was on display in the village and all in the village filed past and paid their respects to her during the farewell ceremony. There was much grief shared with loud wailing by the women. Her body was wrapped in a bark covering tied together with vine stringers. Then she was carried off into the jungle by a group of women who would, I presume, bury her body.

"I am unclear about what I should do now. I feel that my time in this place has now come to a conclusion and I need to move on. But I cannot leave my daughter here. I plan to speak to the elders about leaving and taking her with me so that she can enjoy growing up in a modern society.

"I have wanted to give back to this community and yet all I feel now is that I have robbed them of one of their favourite daughters. My dream of helping this community in return for their gold seems to have turned to nothing. Only memories and stories will remain, I can leave no other footprints.

"As I have learned to love these people, I have also reflected on their values. I cannot but help compare them to my own western values. The gold in the river means nothing to them. The real gold is in this little black bird that has dominated their culture. It appoints leaders, it is revered in language, song, and even in dances that mimic its bobbing movement. It has brought a richness and identity to these people that is far more valuable than any gold. It is such

irony that in the same location where gold and bird dwell, there is such a collision of values between western and indigenous cultures.

"I pray that the leaders of the future will be able to find a way through the maze of confusion that will undoubtedly come as foreigners scramble to get their hands on the gold. I hope so strongly that they will be able to hold onto the richness that their little mascot, nenge, brings into the society. It is a richness that has held them together for generations.

"Life is more than what we can see with our eyes. There is a mystery beyond our sight. Nenge has helped maintain that mystery among the Moiaimba, the knowledge that there is someone else out there who is bigger than the individual, who is worth living for. Nenge points these people to the spiritual reality of a Creator God who loves them and cares for them. Their response in turn is to nurture each other and the land that nenge has shared with them.

"I have seen the bird. I am a believer in nenge. It is real. It is no wonder they have no interest in the gold as we would. They do not fight over specks of gold dust just as they do not fight over the leaves of trees or stones in the river. They have it in abundance already, but it has no place in their culture. It is just there, part of the beautiful scenery they enjoy in this magnificent valley.

"But the nenge is the rarest of all treasures. It is seen so rarely, perhaps once in a decade? Only those who have seen it know of its reality, the rest must believe their story. To protect its sanctity, only those who have seen it know where it lives, and that is a secret to them, 'nenge nematanu', the people of the bird. That name, that elite group of people, conjures up such mystique within the culture, that to destroy the bird would be to destroy the heart of Moiaimba culture, and that would destroy the people.

"I hope and pray that this would not happen, that future leaders will be able at all costs to hold onto what is rich for them and not have it stolen from them."

Two days later grandfather wrote again.

*"I have spoken with the elders. They are sympathetic to
my desire to take my daughter with me. I have told them
that I believe she has a much better future growing up in my
culture where she can gain an education. I am not convinced
that they had a clue what I was talking about, but they did
acknowledge that I knew many things and that she would
be able to learn them as well.*

*"However they wished for me to wait until she is at least
old enough to take some solid foods and not be dependent
on breast milk. I agreed to this as it is best for my little one.*

*"I advised the elders that I will leave in the next few days
and return to Port Moresby. There I will be able to sell my
gold stocks and spend some time integrating back into the
world of my own culture. I will return in about three months
and spend time with them again until my little one is ready
to travel. I suspect that I will be able to come to some
arrangement where I can take several people with me to Port
Moresby, including the nursing mother. This will make sure
the baby is well looked after on the trip. Hopefully it will
also allow a greater understanding of the immediate outside
world for some of them.*

*"My rosewood chair will come with me now and I will
pack and consign it back to Sydney ready for when I
return."*

Several days later, as Grandfather prepared to leave
Mambusu, he talked further with the elders.

*"I spoke at length with Lupiano, my dear wife's father,
and the other elders. It has vexed me that my daughter is
actually the mother of the next headman of Mambusu.
Nenge has revealed himself to every successive headman
when the time was right for his appointment, but they also
are the firstborn son of the wife or daughter of the reigning
headman. By removing my daughter from the community as
I am planning to do, I am removing her ability to perform
that sacred duty, to produce the next leader. I have no wish
to leave the community in this position, or to deny nenge his
sacred role in anointing the next Lupiano.*

"So I have advised the elders that I will ensure that my grandson returns to lead the people. As a mark of that return, I have promised them that the person who returns with the chair will be the next Lupiano.

"It is a bold undertaking I know, and one I know I will have no control over or ability to make happen. So in this I am placing my trust in nenge to fulfill his sacred duty in appointing Lupiano, but also in the Creator God I worship. He is the One who ultimately looks after his people and gives them purpose and fulfillment in life. It is in following his ways that people find happiness in community."

There was noise out in the main room and I heard Kila's voice. Their party had returned and my reading must conclude for now. No doubt the rest of the diary was about grandfather's trip to Moresby and subsequent return to collect his daughter.

As I prepared to meet up with Kila and the team again, I thought about grandfather's words. The relevance of his comments, the insights into the Moiaimba that he had learnt and wrote about, and his courage in stepping out to predict my return, astounded me. Was it a prediction or just a hope? Is there a difference when faith is involved?

He desperately wanted the best for the Moiaimba, and in faith predicted an ending that would, ironically, mean that what he did give back to the community was so valuable even he would not have believed it. It was such a shame that he couldn't see this at the time. But isn't that faith – believing what is possible and trusting God for it to happen?

I wondered who was actually making all this happen. Was it Grandfather's faith, or the God in whom he ultimately trusted, and was *nenge* at work ensuring the survival of this community?

Perhaps it was a combination of all three.

Chapter 29

The Alternatives

Kila was enthusiastic about the day trip to the mine site.

"What an incredibly beautiful place this is, Justin," he said as soon as he saw me. "I can't get over what a paradise it is here."

Lily had prepared a meal expecting the group would be hungry when they got in, and we invited all of them in to join us as they were.

"Well I'm glad you enjoyed the trip, Kila, I'm only sorry I couldn't have been with you. I doubt if my leg'll be strong enough to do that walk for another three months at least."

"No worries Justin," replied Kila, "I took plenty of photos to show you. I don't think we got as far as the aircraft though. The others thought we should turn around sooner or we'd be walking home in the dark."

I turned to look at all the group members and asked, "What are your thoughts then after today?"

"Our minds are struggling to come to grips with the changes that the mine will bring," said David. "That land down there is so much part of our heritage and ancestral stories, it was hard to imagine what it would be like with a mine there."

"I keep wondering if it's really worthwhile," added Hendros the businessman. "I mean if we do a cost-benefit analysis, it really seems like we have to give up a lot, and I don't see that the benefits are worth the cost. Do we have to give up the past to be able to live in the future?"

Paul had a different view, but he was a teacher. "I see the benefits that we're being promised in education for our children," he added. "But I do have a concern that the proposal plans state at least five years before any school is built. I wonder if it'll really happen in that time or whether it'll take longer. That means we will not see educational benefits for a whole generation of primary school children. The other question I have is this - what do we do with a new generation of educated young people? I don't see any guarantees that the mine will employ them. So we end up with more educated but unemployed youth whose education may have alienated them from their traditional values."

David spoke up again. "We've been wrestling with the concept of an alternative to the mine. Kila couldn't stop telling us all day how beautiful our valley was. He feels that a mine could destroy this ecosystem and asked us what flora and fauna we knew of that is unique to the valley. That's something we don't have an answer for. We only know what we have here, we don't really know the value of that, or how unique it may be."

"Do you want to add to that Kila?" I asked.

"Yes, it's true," replied Kila, "I was really struck by the natural beauty of the valley. It's still quite untouched ecologically. I felt like I was in the Garden of Eden or some sort of paradise today. The river is pristine, with beautiful clear water you can drink. We could hear the birds wherever we were. Maybe I've forgotten what bush is because I've been in Moresby too long, but it was beautiful. The thought came to me that there might be potential to use this natural habitat as a commercial opportunity for an eco-project, something that sustains it as it is but generates finances at the same time."

I was very glad for Kila's insights. He'd opened everyone's eyes to other potential commercial but sustainable opportunities.

"Well, Lily and I had an interesting day as well," I said. "We started by laying out the maps again and following the borders of the land the mining company has its eyes on. As an aside I plotted the gold vein, then the crash site and my rescue site. Here is the map." I held up the map we'd marked with Xs. "Then, by chance really, I marked where I thought I'd seen the bird…. sorry Kila, we are talking about secret Moiaimba customs here so I ask for your total confidentiality…. and when I plotted it, we realized that it's in the same place as the gold vein."

"We've known the bird lives in that area, Lupiano," confirmed David, "but didn't realize it was right where the gold source is. That's a real revelation for us now."

I continued. "I'm sorry to reveal what has been a tribal secret for so long. We don't have to disclose this location outside of this meeting. However we now have a choice. If we agree to the mine, then the *nenge* and its habitat will be wiped out. If the value of preserving the bird and its habitat is more important to the Moiaimba than the value of the gold, then we must ensure the mine does not go ahead.

"It seems to me that the real gold for the Moiaimba is the value of the *nenge*. So I think the bird has made our decision for us."

After a few moments of silence, David spoke up again.

"Once again you are demonstrating the wisdom of a true leader, Lupiano. I believe that this wisdom has been given to you from others. You're entirely correct in all you say. For all these years, the *nenge* has lived on top of the gold. While we had no value for the gold, the *nenge* is of such value to us as a culture that its demise would be the demise of our people. We cannot entertain such a thing happening. We cannot allow the mine to come to Mambusu."

The others nodded in agreement. No further discussion was needed. David was right. My wisdom had come from my grandfather and the bird itself, but the story of that would be left for another day.

"Kila, your ideas are very helpful," I said to the group. "What possibilities do you think there are for establishing a reserve which would ensure no one can mine the area? Could we actually make the area a habitat for the *nenge*?"

Some ideas were starting to float around in our heads now.

"I don't see why that couldn't be done. If there are any endangered species there, you'd have a strong case. What's this bird you refer to? Is that the same as the *nenge*?" asked Kila.

"Yes, they're the same," I replied. "It's a Bird of Paradise referred to as the Six Plumed Bird of Paradise or Lawes Parotia. It's sacred to that area and has a vital role to play in the cultural heritage of the Moiaimba people. It's like an icon to them. I can't tell you anymore because the stories are sacred to the elders of the Moiaimba."

"Well there you have it, a sanctuary for the *nenge*," said Kila.

It was Lily's turn to ask a question. "Kila, do you think the area would be attractive for tourists if we created a hotel or lodge at the river junction? Then tourists could go on guided walks through the bush and see the wildlife firsthand. Do you think that would work?" she asked.

Kila replied, "Certainly, I don't see why it wouldn't work. I mean there is a growing interest in eco-tourism these days. People want to see the real PNG, not just mass produced artifacts coated in boot polish to look old."

Kila thought for few seconds before continuing.

"You have a number of things going which combined could be quite lucrative for you while all working together to actually preserve your heritage. I mean you could still use the gold in the river even if you create a sanctuary for the *nenge*. There will still be people who want to come and pan for gold downstream. That could even be part of a tourism package. You know, 'Pan for gold, guaranteed results – you keep half and donate half back to the sanctuary'. I think you could do that under an Alluvial Mining Lease that would not be detrimental to the environment or the creation of a wildlife sanctuary."

I saw some smiles start to creep onto the otherwise serious faces. Kila's mind was into overdrive now, but the ideas he was expressing were having a profound impact on the group. For the first time someone was engaging them in a creative thinking process with real possibilities for the future.

"This is all great," said Hendros, "but where do we get the funds to do something like this. You're talking about a wildlife sanctuary, a tourist lodge, improved roads and airstrip…. I mean all this needs money to develop. Even the Mambusu Guest Haus has struggled along barely making enough to keep the hot water going…"

"And sometimes not even that!" I muttered quietly.

I thought it was time that I let the group know of another decision I had recently come to.

"It's very encouraging that we're now moving to a place of creative thinking about possibilities for the future without a mine. We must keep thinking this way until we find the best combination of ideas that we can move ahead with.

"In the meantime, I believe that we need to commence a fund that will provide the financial undergirding for our future. The Member's Moi Futures, wherever he is getting his money from, is obviously tied up by the Member. I have no desire to use that fund. It may well be the subject of corruption enquiries in future as well. So I have an announcement to make.

"I'm donating my government service retirement fund, once I have built a house for Lily and me in Mambusu, to start the Nenge Heritage Foundation. I'll be asking Kila if he can make the arrangements to register this as a trust fund when he gets back to Port Moresby."

The group began to applaud and there were nods and smiles among them that made it very clear they fully supported this initiative. I continued, slowly looking at each person as I addressed them.

"This Foundation will have a Board and all its dealings will be fully transparent. I want it to be a model of good governance. Paul, I'd like to ask you to be Secretary of the Board... Hendros, the Treasurer... Lily, the Legal Officer... David, the Community Liaison Officer... and John, Local Government Liaison Officer. I'll Chair the Board." I paused while each of the new Board members took in what I'd just asked of them, then continued.

"I'd also like to invite Kila, with the approval of the other Board members, to join us as a Director and National Government Liaison Officer. Are there any questions?" I asked in conclusion.

There were several of course, and we discussed in more detail how such a Board would operate, and some of the financial and legal issues in setting up a trust fund. In the end Kila declined the invitation to become a Director, with everyone's full support, because he didn't want to be in a conflict of interest situation as Chief Warden, though he did agree to come on board once the legal situation with the issue of mining leases, whatever the outcome, had been finalized.

As our extended meal drew to a close, the group, now the new Board of the Nenge Heritage Foundation, appeared to be in good spirits. Today had introduced fresh ideas and innovative structures and all felt very encouraged that we were making good progress. But one uncertainty still stood in our pathway.

"Tomorrow," I announced, "as a group we must commit ourselves to going through the list of names on the Member's list. We mustn't forget that we have five days left in which to deny the Member his lease. Tomorrow we must find at least two names on the list that don't fit. If not, then we'll have to explore the possibility of irregularities in the Member's conduct especially in regard to any of his activities that might be in conflict with the requirements of the Mining Act. Then we can start to relax and plan our future. We meet here at 9 am. Thank you, my brothers and sister."

Chapter 30

The Sting

The next day we were all assembled at 9.00 am. We separated out those names that we had no doubt about as being genuine Mambusu area landowners, and those that needed further checking. Out of the Member's list of forty-one, we found nine that needed further checking, and that led us to a final list of four that we could confirm were invalid names.

They were of the Member, Honourable Lupo Warina Udio MP, or whatever configuration of that name he used, his representative in Mambusu, and two others. The last two were confirmed 100% as Deria landowners with no claim to land in Mambusu. They were also not in attendance at the Member's meeting.

The next step was to follow through with the legal proceedings and have the Lease Agreement stopped. Lily offered to drive back to Port Moresby the next day with Kila and together they'd make sure the Member was caught in his own trap. They'd hire additional lawyers if required.

By now I was fairly mobile on my crutches and knew that others in the community would take care of me. Grandfather had assured me of that community care when it was needed. So I thought it would be a good idea for Lily to get a few days in Port Moresby, see her brothers and sister there, and perhaps do some more homework on eco-enterprises which might work for the Moiaimba.

As they were about to leave Mambusu, Kila received a phone call.

"Hello, yes Member, this is Kila," he answered. A pause while he listened, then replied, "Oh, I'm very sorry you've had trouble contacting me. I've been at Mambusu for the last three days – didn't my staff advise you that?" I knew full well that Kila had told his staff that they were not to disclose where he'd gone to anyone, including politicians!

"Yes," continued Kila, "I thought I should come out here and see what's going on firsthand. I heard reports that there was some dissension at your meeting here so thought I should come and investigate. I was concerned that Justin Orlando was not doing his job satisfactorily, Member."

The Member was furious. "Secretary, it is not acceptable that you are away from your office and visiting my electorate without my knowledge. When are you coming back to Moresby?" he demanded.

"Actually Member," replied Kila, "I'm just about to leave now to drive back, so I should be in by nightfall."

"Good, then I want a full report of your findings at Mambusu on my desk by 10 am tomorrow," the Member continued to demand.

"Honourable Member, I regret to advise you that I'm not able to meet that deadline. However I suggest that we schedule a meeting for two days' time when I'll have a full report, and I can brief you face to face," replied Kila.

The Member wasn't happy but had to concede to this arrangement. After hanging up the phone, Kila turned to Lily and I and said, "I have two days to set the trap for the Member. Lily, can you attend that briefing with the Member and I as well?"

"Yes, that'd be an honour," replied Lily, smiling again. I could see she'd relish the opportunity to spring a trap on the Member and turn the tables on him.

The next day they presented their findings to the court registrar in preparation for the next hearing, which would be the day after meeting the Member. Kila had very wisely kept the Moi Futures cheque and hadn't banked it yet. He'd also kept the two pigs safe. While both had been given to him, he'd claim he hadn't actually accepted them, and was only holding them in safekeeping. He hoped that they could be used as evidence against the Member. With a mounting case of fraud against the Member, they also filed papers to charge him concurrent with the expectation of a victory over the land lease list.

Finding the link between Namel Mining and Moi Futures was needed. We were all sure that Moi Futures must be receiving its funds from Namel Mining, but the Member had so far been able to hide that link. If Lily and Kila could prove that the Member had used Namel Mining funds to bribe Kila, they had the basis for a fraud case against him. Once the court papers were lodged, they had a day to find that link.

Lily also had a list of people she wanted to contact who may be able to help her understand some of the alternative eco-based possibilities for their area. She wanted to follow up seriously with several wildlife conservation groups to see their interest in working with the Nenge Heritage Foundation. While protecting the little bird was the foremost ambition, there were also other Birds of Paradise in the area. She knew that further up the mountain past Deria as well as upstream from the gold site there were also habitats for other species of this famous bird.

She'd also heard that funding for infrastructure such as schools and health facilities might be available from major western country funding organizations when land is used for nature conservation instead of resource depletion. She'd make some contacts to follow these possibilities.

Lily was sure that some ecological studies must have been done in the area over the years, but the community had no information on them. So she booked a visit to the University of PNG to find out what other species of flora and fauna that existed in Moiaimba land were listed as endangered or rare. If a wildlife reserve was created then it may also provide a site for the universities to conduct wildlife research.

She knew that several tourism companies advertised eco-friendly tourism and wished to contact them to discuss such possibilities at Mambusu. Tourists were willing to pay top dollars for a truly natural PNG experience. That could include forest and river walking tours, even two and three day hikes further up into the mountain areas, sighting Birds of Paradise in the bush, or down the river to the coast, living in villages along the way.

With ideas still about using the gold in the river as another source of income, she wanted to assess what a gold panning experience for tourists would look like. She needed discussions with PNG Tourism and like-minded groups who could see the potential and how it could be realized. A small collection point for alluvial gold that allowed visitors in restricted numbers to pan for gold downstream was part of the consideration.

It had also been suggested that the climate in Mambusu might be ideally suited to crops that could yield an agriculturally based income for the area. While cardamom had been grown successfully in places like the Managalasi plateau on the northern side of the Owen Stanley Ranges, Mambusu was a similar climate and altitude. She knew there were many species of orchids also found in the area. So she wanted to spend some time in discussion with Department of Agriculture officials.

For all the Nenge Heritage Foundation team, their world of ideas had suddenly been expanded and there seemed no end to the possibilities now. It would be a busy time in Port Moresby for Lily and Kila.

The Member had requested they meet at Sandy's Bar & Restaurant in Boroko, obviously his favourite haunt. Expecting that he'd be meeting with Kila alone again, he was surprised to see Lily there as well.

"Member, Lily is accompanying me as legal representative for the Mambusu community," Kila said as he introduced her to the Member. Of course, he knew who she was – the girl from the Guest Haus – but was surprised to find out that she was also a lawyer. It may have given him the first hint that something was wrong.

The Member barged ahead anyway with his agenda. "Well, if she must be here then, sit down both of you," he said, and motioned to two chairs at the table for four.

"Well Kila, what can you tell me about things at Mambusu? I thought this fellow Orlando was injured in the accident and flown out of Mambusu. I said I wanted him out of the way, so why is he back again now, on crutches I hear? He's stirred up things against the mine proposal. I'm preparing deportation papers for him now."

At news of this development Lily sat forward in her chair and was about to defend Justin, but Kila quietly and unobtrusively motioned with his hand for her to sit back again. This wasn't an argument she needed to win, but the Member had certainly got her fired up very quickly.

"Member, you're correct in what you say," replied Kila, "he was injured in the plane crash and came out of Mambusu just before you arrived. I would have appreciated your thanks for this. I got him out of the way before you arrived, just as you asked me."

Kila and Lily knew that was not exactly true but it added weight to Kila's argument.

He continued, "However on the matter of his return to Mambusu, I'm afraid that Mr Orlando was free to choose where he wished to recuperate, in liaison with his doctors of course. I have no power to stop him being back in Mambusu, especially now that he has resigned from the Department." Kila knew that news would add some spice to the discussion.

"What, he's resigned? On what grounds? Is he going back to Australia now then?" asked the Member.

"No Member, in fact exactly the opposite. He's going to stay in Mambusu and work in the community there," replied Kila.

"Well that's easily fixed. He'll be deported in a matter of days," said the Member.

Kila followed this trail a little further. "On what grounds will you have him deported?" he asked.

"Kila, you know as well as I do that a foreigner cannot enter into politics. His action in stirring up the community against the mine site, which is this government's policy, is involvement in politics. He's gone." The Member was very sure about his tactic.

Lily spoke now. "Honourable Member. I need to make you aware that Mr Orlando has applied for Citizenship. As you know he's held a visa as a fully contracted long-term public servant. He's now upgraded that to apply for Citizenship. His application has been formally approved by the Secretary for Foreign Affairs & Migration and his citizenship will be issued any day now."

Lily recalled in her mind how we'd discussed the issue of my status in PNG the day after my operation, and I'd decided that if my future was as Lupiano, then I must become a PNG Citizen. Lily had submitted my paperwork before we flew back to Mambusu. We were able to short cut what may have taken months of processing to just a few days. As a senior manager in the public service, I had many friends in other departments who were more than willing to make sure the application landed on the right person's desk very quickly!

The Member's face dropped at this news. He knew he'd have no power to change that decision now. Mr Orlando was here to stay.

"Honourable Member," spoke Lily again. "I must also inform you of another significant matter in regard to the lease of Mambusu land for the Namel Mining Pty Ltd venture. The Agreement states that there must be at least forty landowners sign or the lease cannot proceed."

"That's correct," butted in the Member, "and we got that number to sign up. If your Mr Citizen Orlando hadn't interfered, we would have had lots more sign it!"

"Mr Warina," said Lily quite firmly again, "we've screened all of the forty-one signatories on your list. As you know, the court injunction was imposed to allow that process to occur."

The Member butted in again, "Unnecessary interference once again by Orlando and his men, and a totally uncalled for court injunction." The Member was not a happy man, and had overlooked the fact that Orlando's men included a woman!

Lily continued. "Mr Warina, I'm advising you that at least four of your forty one signatories are illegal. There may be others as well but your list of signatories is invalid. The Agreement cannot proceed."

The Member was furious. This time he didn't care who was listening at Sandy's Bar & Restaurant.

"What right do you have to come in here and accuse me of forging that document, young miss!" he shouted at her. "You'd be better back at Mambusu serving saksak than coming in here and insulting a Member of Parliament, your member at that!"

Lily knew that the Member had developed a bad temper. She also knew that he used it as a tool to intimidate and manipulate people. But Lily was not among those who were intimidated by this kind of tactic, and she calmly responded to the Member.

"Member, your name is the first one in question. You have signed as Udio W. Whether you claim this is yours or a relatives doesn't matter. The fact is that the Udio clan does not have any landholdings at Mambusu. Your attempt to bring the numbers up to forty-one using your own family name is fraudulent. You don't qualify." Lily made the case quite clear to the Member, who'd gone silent now. She continued.

"Your assistant also doesn't qualify. There are two other names of Deria people who were neither present at the meeting nor have land holdings in Mambusu. I have their names here if you'd like me to read them out," said Lily calmly.

"What are you people trying to do to me?" the Member yelled. He knew he was beaten but only knew how to react in anger.

"This means that at the court hearing tomorrow, your land lease deal will be declared invalid. The mining proposal will not be proceeding," said Lily.

"Mr Woro," said the Member as he turned his attention to Kila in disgust, "you are Secretary of a government department. I expected more from you and I'm disappointed that you appear to have presided over this turn of events that's contrary to the government's intentions. The government wants that mine to go ahead, do you understand? Your position is tenuous. Unless you can change these circumstances so that the mine proceeds, you will be charged with fraud. You know what I'm talking about." Once again the Member was trying to gain the upper hand.

Kila had more ammunition up his sleeve but wasn't going to fire it here. It would wait for another day. Tomorrow they would face each other in court and then we'd see who had the most powerful bullets. So he just looked the Member in the eye and nodded. Yes, he was very aware of what the Member was talking about.

"Member, may I ask you a question please?" asked Kila, and then proceeded to ask without waiting for the Member to approve.

"If we can change this ruling or find another mechanism for the mine to proceed, will the financial structure remain the same? I'm in no hurry to lose my job and have my reputation at stake. So can you help me understand how the financial structure will work? I think that there wasn't enough explanation about this when you were in Mambusu, so people were confused," said Kila. Lily recognised that he was sweet talking the Member, trying to pull him onside again, though she wasn't sure why.

"Now that's a better way to approach this," responded the Member in a more conciliatory tone of voice. "Let's look for ways to make it happen. We can easily forget the little episode with the signatories list, can't we?

"Now, let's see, it's as I said, Namel Mining had legal advice recommending setting up Namel Community Trust to receive all monies for the community. They appointed me as Chairman, which is only appropriate given I'm the headman of the Moiaimba."

Kila had a quick glance at Lily who was already watching for his reaction. It would be a difficult blow for the Member when he discovered he was no longer the headman!

"And Member, you would be in charge of disbursement of these funds to the community?" asked Kila.

"Yes, that's right my friend," replied the Member. "I will personally oversight distribution of funds back into the community."

"Has Namel Mining made any financial commitment to the trust fund then, to help kick it off?" asked Kila. Lily was starting to see where he was going with this questioning.

"Oh yes, definitely. I was able to lobby them to deposit two million US dollars into the account. Great work I thought." The Member was very willing to boast of his accomplishments, something Kila was using for his undoing.

"Member, well done," said Kila as he reached across the table to shake the Member's hand. Another little step in opening up the Member by using his own vanity.

"So I presume that money is ready to use now then? You see I didn't realize things were so far advanced. I wish you'd told me earlier," said Kila. "Have you had any expenses then from the trust account?"

"Oh yes, I've been able to use nearly 100,000 kina so far. You know, all expenses to help move the project along," replied the Member. He thought for a second and then continued, walking right into the trap.

"You know some of the expenses, such as yours, need to be handled sensitively but are really essential to the wellbeing of the mine."

Kila saw his opening, and replied, "Oh, so the Moi Futures account is the one you are using to disburse funds?"

Before he'd realized it, the Member had replied, "Yes that's it." He looked at Kila and the realization of what he had said began to sink in.

"It's all legitimate and above board, as I told you before, nothing wrong with using that account," said the Member, trying to justify his fraudulent bank account.

Kila had planned to use his ammunition in court the next day, and held to that conviction. So he would end this conversation amicably and not arouse the Member's suspicion any more than had been done already. He hoped that the Member's target today was Lily and not himself.

"So as I understand the situation," Kila summarized, "the court proceedings tomorrow will hear Lily's evidence that the list of forty signatures is invalid and stop the current mine proceedings. However we can, I'm sure, begin to look for other ways to continue the mine proposal. So we'll meet you at the Court House tomorrow and get this procedure behind us."

Kila wanted the Member to feel a bit more relaxed about the case. He couldn't win it but he was keen to try and find a way around it, and Kila played that game with him.

"You should be a lawyer," Lily said to Kila as they left Sandy's Bar & Restaurant, after paying the bill for the Member.

That evening Lily called me and briefed me on the events in Port Moresby, especially pleased that the link between the Namel Community Trust and Moi Futures Ltd had been established. Bank records would verify the transfer of funds now that the identity of both accounts was linked.

Chapter 31

The Fall

Next day the Court met nearly an hour after it was scheduled due to the late arrival of the presiding judge. But then things moved along smoothly as Lily presented her evidence concerning the false signatories. The judge proceeded to declare the Member's list invalid, which halted the land lease process. The mine would not proceed – at least for now.

Following straight on from this though, much to the Member's surprise, was the case against him. Lily had prepared well and presented the various cases against him.

- He had fraudulently signed his name on the list of landowners to boost the numbers, knowing that he was not a landowner at Mambusu.

- He had established a company and bank account, Moi Futures Ltd, without the authority of the Namel Community Trust Board, to fraudulently use Namel Community Trust fund monies. Namel Mining Pty Ltd also joined as a party to this case against the Member.

- He had sought to bribe the Secretary of the Department of Social Resources by paying for the Secretary's costs to build his own house using a Moi Futures Ltd cheque, and by supplying two pigs purchased by Moi Futures Ltd.

As evidence, Kila had produced the Moi Futures cheque, and then caused a stir in the courtroom by bringing in the two large pigs. He somewhat contemptuously added the comment that he'd fattened them further so they should return a nice profit!

In handing down his ruling, the judge noted that the Member had acted in a manner that brought disgrace to the Parliament. He'd not met his duty of care to his constituency, and was charged with fraud. While he was referred to the Leadership Tribunal, the Judge suspended him from any further dealings that involved the Namel mine proposal, banning him from holding any office as a Director or Chairman in those companies.

The tables had been turned. But there was one further piece of information that the Member needed to know. Lily waited for a disheveled Lupo Warina to exit the court building.

"I'll get my revenge on your Mr Orlando, young miss," he growled at Lily as he approached her.

"Mr Warina," responded Lily, still calm and collected, "I need to tell you something important. You know the stories about the gold prospector who married the headman's daughter?"

"Are you crazy, girl," replied the Member, "what on earth are you talking about? Of course I know the stories, everyone does, but they're of no relevance here."

Lily continued. "You need to know that the prospector's daughter, the one he took away with him, had a son in Australia. That son has returned to PNG. His Australian name is Justin Orlando."

The Member was speechless and just stared at Lily hardly willing to believe what he was hearing.

"His grandfather gave him another name, and that is the name we now know him by. Mr Orlando is Lupiano," said Lily.

As if to reinforce what she'd just said, she added, "He has returned to lead his people, the Moiaimba people. You'll do well from now on to respect him."

The colour drained from the Member's face and he sat down on the Court House steps. If he was surprised by events in the courtroom, they were nothing compared with this news. Not only had he lost his credibility as the Member, but he'd now lost any claim to be the leader of the Moiaimba. He would go back to Sandy's Bar & Restaurant and find a quiet table by himself while he pondered his humiliation.

Chapter 32

The Curse

Lily stayed in Port Moresby for another few days before returning to Mambusu. She was loaded up with papers, brochures and ideas from her visits to the various people she'd seen about developing sustainable and commercial eco-friendly ventures.

The first evening back at Mambusu we talked for hours over the possibilities. There was no doubt in our minds that the Moiaimba were entering a new future without the mine, or at least without the mining company. Yet it was a future that seemed to hold so much more hope because they were in charge of their own destiny.

"Lily," I said at one stage, "can you tell me why your grandfather was excluded from the eldership of the Moiaimba?"

"Oh, I didn't think you knew about that," she said, somewhat surprised. "It happened after your grandfather had seen the *nenge*. Your grandfather didn't know that it was a secret in our society and so he told my grandfather about it. They were good friends then. By hearing about it and not seeing the bird himself though, my grandfather came under our customs that said that he could never become an elder. It's something that lives in our family now. It means neither I nor my brothers can ever be an elder."

"Lily, I need to read you the story from my grandfather's diary," I said. I turned to where grandfather had written of this is his diary.

"Your grandfather's name was Seri, wasn't it?"

She nodded.

I read to her the story of my grandfather's anguish because he'd told Seri the sacred story of his encounter with the *nenge*, and his desire to help Seri through the tragic consequences of his ignorance of their customs.

"Today when Seri returned, I told him of what I had seen, still absolutely enthralled by the display. His reaction was most unexpected. His face, even though dark skinned, almost went pale, his expression became serious and he looked quite stunned. He staggered back a little and then sat down, staring at me.

"'Seri, are you ok?' I asked him in Moi language.

"He was silent. I was baffled by his reaction and could not understand at all why my story of the bird had shocked him.

"After a while he said to me, 'Adi, you must speak with my father.'

"With that Seri withdrew and kept himself aloof from me, as if he was fearful of me, or that there was now something between us which had tempered his behaviour towards me. The jovial Seri had gone.

"I have no idea what has happened here and so I must get back to the village tomorrow to speak with Seri's father and get to the bottom of it. My relationship with the men has been seriously affected. I wonder if I have done something to upset the balance of my relationship with these people?"

I was careful not to reveal the story of the bird to Lily so skipped to grandfather's final comments about Seri after he'd talked with the elders.

"I was speechless. No wonder Seri was also shocked because he must have realized the significance of my story. I

was describing something to him that was taboo, sacred, unspeakable, except for those who have seen it themselves. Seri was now caught in a struggle of being exposed to something regarded as so secret in his culture. I felt for him and knew I would have to somehow help him through this."

"I believe that my grandfather was never able to resolve this with your grandfather, is that true?" I asked Lily.

"Yes, that's right," she replied, "their friendship was never the same. My grandfather had to respect your grandfather as an elder but could never attain that himself because of your grandfather's mistake."

"Lily, my dear, in a few weeks we are going to be married. This legacy from my grandfather is like a curse on your family. He left Mambusu so disappointed because he felt he hadn't been able to give back to the community what he'd hoped."

Lily was listening to me, soaking up all that I was saying.

I continued, "The elders have recognised your leadership abilities but because of this curse they can't appoint you to be an elder. I've come to realize that in fact grandfather has given back to this community what it needed most. My return as Lupiano has brought a new hope to the community at a time they need it most. You told me yourself that people trust me. There's nothing more precious than that, and that's what grandfather has now been able to give back, through me."

I paused to collect my thoughts and then continued.

"Through our marriage, we are rejoining the relationship between our families that was broken by our grandparents. Do you see that? Just as your grandfather was prohibited from becoming an elder through the old laws of your customs, so we'll break that curse by entering into a new legal contract, our marriage relationship together, one of commitment and trust.

"You won't have to live under the spell of the old law anymore. Under the new contract, you'll be free to take up that mantle of eldership with me. This will be the final legacy of my grandfather through me, to restore the relationship with Seri, with his clan, to break the curse."

I couldn't describe it any clearer than that. The fulfillment of grandfather's deepest wishes to give back to the Moiaimba was now complete.

We sat spellbound for some minutes as Lily contemplated what it would mean for her family to live now without that legacy. How it would free them to enter into community life again knowing they were once again whole people, fully able to exercise their gifts in leadership, and fully recognised for who they are.

As we sat together, she gently placed her hand in mine. Tears welled up in her eyes. She was free. Soon she would be Lupiano's wife. Soon she could be '*nenge nematane*'.

With eyes still wet and a tear running down her cheek she looked up at me, a cheeky grin on her face, and said,

"How about you tell me the story about that little bird now?"

———————

Postscript

The *Six Plumed* or *Six Wired Bird of Paradise,* also called *Lawes's Parotia,* is a real bird, one of the magnificent Bird of Paradise species found in Papua New Guinea prized for its plumage used in traditional headdresses.

Video footage of this bird and its unique dance can be found at several YouTube sites by searching its name.

However, there is no Namel Province and there is no Moiaimba tribe or town of Mambusu in Papua New Guinea. There is no Department of Social Resources or Member for Moi or Kila Woro. Justin Orlando and his grandfather also exist only in the pages of this book.

If any names in this story bear a resemblance to any actual persons or places, it is purely coincidental. The words 'moi' and 'nenge' are common in a number of Melanesian and other languages and their use in this story is not representative of any of them. If the use of these or any other word in this story causes offence, I assure that it is unintentional and offer my apologies.

While the characters in this story are fictitious, I have tried to maintain historical and socio-cultural accuracy within the story. I am sure readers, especially those who are familiar with PNG, will identify with the characters, places and issues as if they were real, while recognizing those that in fact, are real.

This story is Book One of the NENGE SERIES. Book Two is titled THE POWER OF THE BIRD.

About the Author

Mike Jelliffe and his wife have lived in PNG on and off since 1971 and raised their three children there. Mike has worked mainly in aviation as a pilot and manager, and in training roles in churches. Having lived in remote locations and towns in both highlands and lowlands provinces across PNG, he has a wide appreciation of PNG local cultures. This is his first novel.

Your feedback on this story is welcomed. This book is available through bookstores or can be ordered direct from the publisher.

Email to: **nengebooks1@gmail.com**
Website: www.nengebooks.com